SURGEON TO THE SIOUX

SURGEON TO THE SIOUX

ROBERT J. STEELMAN

70318

DOUBLEDAY & COMPANY, INC.

GARDEN CITY, NEW YORK

1979

All the characters in this book are fictitious,
and any resemblance to actual persons,
living or dead,
except for historical personages,
is purely coincidental.

Library of Congress Cataloging in Publication Data
Steelman, Robert J
Surgeon to the Sioux.
1. Oglala Indians—Fiction. I. Title.
PZ4.S8145Sv [PS3569.T33847] 813'.5'4
ISBN: 0-385-14430-X
Library of Congress Catalog Card Number 78-22799

"If I were an Indian, I often think I would greatly prefer to cast my lot among those of my people who adhered to the free open plains, rather than submit to the confined limits of a reservation, there to be the recipient of the blessed benefits of civilization, with its vices thrown in without stint or measure.

"Stripped of the beautiful romance with which we have long been so willing to envelop him, the Indian forfeits his claim to the appellation of 'the noble red man.' We see him as he is, a 'savage' in every sense of the word; not worse, perhaps, than his white brother would be, similarly born and bred, but one whose cruel and ferocious nature far exceeds that of any wild beast of the desert.

"When the soil which he has claimed and hunted over for so long a time is demanded by this to him insatiable monster (civilization), there is no appeal; he must yield, or it will roll mercilessly over him, destroying as it advances. Destiny seems to have so willed it, and the world nods its approval."

My Life on the Plains
George Armstrong Custer
University of Nebraska Press, 1966

SURGEON TO THE SIOUX

CHAPTER 1

When he returned from delivering Minnie Almayer's baby out in
Elk Valley, Sam Blair had only a sack of pears for his trouble, although Jake promised to pay him a little cash when he made a
crop. After having been up all night with a stubborn baby girl who
insisted on coming out of Minnie feetfirst, Sam was exhausted. It
was almost noon when he hailed the ferry and drove his old mare,
Thelma, and sagging trap across the river to the Landing.

Fitch's Landing was a sprawl of abandoned storefronts, shacks,
and lean-tos. Once there had been considerably more: saloons,
gambling halls, cribs and brothels with painted women. Now most
of the inhabitants had hurried off to the Black Hills for the new
gold strike there. The Landing had dwindled considerably from the
promising settlement Sam had once hoped would support his practice.

The *Far West* was tied up at the dock, the only steamer bother-
ing to come upriver as far as Fitch's Landing. This was probably
the last trip before the snows came to the Territory. Morose, Sam
unhitched Thelma and put a measure of oats in her feedbag. Then
he walked to the front of the shabby structure of unpainted boards
that served as his office. A faded gilt sign said, SAMUEL PENROSE
BLAIR, M.D.—MEDICINE AND SURGERY. A cot behind a baize curtain
served as a bedroom, and he took most of his meals at Ma Bidwell's
boarding house, across the way.

Cletus Wiley was sitting in the office, eating an apple from a
bushel of fly-specked transparents Sam had taken in for setting old
Charlie Daigle's broken arm. The air was filled with the sweetish
aroma, laced with chicken feathers and the tang of smoked hams. If
barter were cash, Sam Blair would be a wealthy man.

"Chickens was carryin' on something awful a while ago," Cletus volunteered, gnawing at the apple with his few remaining teeth. "I bought a dime's worth of corn at the mill and quieted 'em down. Didn't want 'em upsettin' your patients."

Cletus was an old man in soiled buckskins—one-time miner, one-time gambler, sometime civilian scout for Major Henry Cushing at Fort Pike, many times married—the last time, he claimed, to a Brulé Sioux female up on the Musselshell. He was fond of women, though he complained to Sam his powers were failing. Sam Blair, Cletus was convinced, had somewhere in his armamentarium of pills, powders, and drafts a remedy to restore waning potency.

"Thanks," Sam said. "Charge you a dime for that apple, Cletus, and we come out even."

The patients were two: a drover with a boil on his neck and a young cavalry trooper whom Sam had been treating for the scabies. The drover paid him fifty cents with another fifty on account. The towheaded young trooper, a German boy named Luther Speck, brought him no fee. Luther was covered under Sam's thirty-dollar-a-month contract with Fort Pike to treat their cases, the post being too small to have a doctor. After Sam had coated the affected areas with sulphur and carbolate of tar, bandaged them, and given Luther a bottle of blood and liver tonic, Luther still lingered.

"And remember not to scratch," Sam instructed. "Scratching just spreads the itching."

"What does the tonic do?" Luther wanted to know.

"Purifies the blood, dissolves poisons out of the liver. That's what the scabies is, you know, Luther—bodily poisons coming out through the skin."

"Ought to stay away from Bertha Rambouillet's girls, Luther," Cletus joked.

The young man turned red. "I don't never go there, Cletus; you know that!" Awkwardly he turned to Sam, taking a packet of papers from his coat. "Doc, I don't read too good, and I can't hardly write my name, but you're an eddicated man. Maybe you can help me with this pension stuff."

Sam wiped the sticky tar from his hands. "*You* want a pension, Luther?"

"Not me—my ma! See, Pa was killed at Chancellorsville. Ever since, I been trying to get a pension for Ma. But all they do is send me these papers I don't understand. Lieutenant Wyatt out at the post says he's too busy to bother, and meanwhiles there's Ma back in Pottstown, Pennsylvania, without enough to pay her rent, though I send her every dollar I can manage!"

Sam knew Andy Wyatt. Lieutenant Andrew Aylesworth Wyatt was a ginger-haired young West Pointer, the chief rival to Sam Blair for Clara Freeman's affections. With a sigh, Sam sat down and examined the papers.

"Well," he said after a while, "I don't see it's too difficult. They just want you to file again. They say they lost some of the papers. Then there were some dates of service for your pa and also your mother's birth date you didn't give them."

Luther swallowed, hopefully. "Could you—would you—"

Bone-weary after a sleepless night, Sam filled out the forms for him, wrote a brief covering note, witnessed Luther's signature, and handed him the packet.

"I'll never be able to thank you enough, Doc!" the young man enthused. "You don't know what this means to me—and Ma! You're just about the best doctor and finest man I know!"

Embarrassed, Sam hurried him to the door.

"Mail come up for you on the *Far West*," Cletus said.

Sam knew what was in the bundle, but went through it anyway. There were statements of unpaid debt from the wholesale drug company in St. Louis; from the Springfield Academy of Medicine for his final year's board bill and tuition; from Professor Elton Perkins for the complete set of "Perkins' Famous Magnetic Tractors, with Electrical Dynamo, Electrodes, Conducting Salves, and Anatomical Charts with Recommended Points of Application—Thirty-Five Dollars and Fifty Cents Less 2% For Cash." Appended to the bill was Professor Perkins' anguished personal note:

> Dr., I can not continue to manufacture my Quality Instrument unless Deadbeats like You pay up. Please remit at Once or I will be Forced to take Steps.

Sam rubbed his forehead. Foolishly, perhaps, he had bought the expensive Tractors as the latest advance in the healing arts. Now he couldn't pay for them. Things were necking down to a mighty small hole.

"Doc," Cletus said, "I worry about you drivin' all over Elk Valley in that danged trap. You ain't even got a weapon."

"No one bothers me," Sam said, throwing the bills in the peach basket that served for rubbish.

The old man took out an ancient six-shot percussion revolver, sighting along the barrel at a cockroach. "Traded a Ree for this old Starr blunderbuss. I'd admire for you to take it along with you when you go out on calls, especial down the valley and around Rainy Butte. There's a passel of young Oglala bucks feelin' their oats lately, and—"

"Thanks, Cletus," Sam said, "but I'd probably shoot myself in the foot. In the war I never hit a single reb."

The old man shrugged, put the gun away. "Leastways, you could get rid of your old plug, Thelma, and that wheel-sprung trap and ride a horse instead. That way maybe you kin outrun some red critter that's anxious for your hair."

Sam brushed back the long-uncut hair. "I've got no quarrel with the Indians. In a way—though I'm careful of how I speak about it around here—this land used to belong to them anyhow. I don't think they intend me any harm."

Cletus tucked a wad of tobacco into his cheek, his nose and whiskered chin almost meeting over the scanty-toothed mouth. "Suit y'self!" he grumbled. "I was only thinkin' of your own good, Doc!"

"I'm sorry," Sam apologized. "I didn't mean to be ungrateful. It's just—I guess I'm just a little discouraged today." Shaking his head, he looked at the welter of papers, medicines, bills, bartered produce, the broken window he had been intending to fix.

Cletus cackled. "Sounds like woman trouble to me. You and Clara Freeman have another fight? I hear Andy Wyatt's been sparkin' her lately."

"What the hell do I care about Andy Wyatt?" Sam snapped. "That damned tin soldier, with his fancy ways!" Then, feeling he was being graceless, his eye lit on the Magnetic Tractors in their plush-lined case. "With you, Cletus," he said, "everything is reducible to women! Well, maybe you're right." Taking out the polished electrodes of the Tractors, he connected the wires to the

Electrical Dynamo. "Tell you what I'm going to do. I'm grateful for your concern, and to prove it I'm going to give you a treatment."

Cletus' bushy eyebrows wigwagged in concern. "What kind of a treatment?"

Sam scanned Professor Perkins' manual. "Well, for just about anything that ails you! Constipation, liver complaints, dyspepsia, scrofula, catarrhs, consumption, general debility—"

"What's that last?"

"General debility."

"Ain't that what I got, Doc? Last time at Bertha Rambouillet's place I couldn't hardly—"

"I know," Sam said. "I'm only going to give you a light treatment." Attaching the meter to read the Electric Charge, he added, "If the treatment agrees with you, I'll try a heavier charge next time." He handed Cletus the electrodes. "Now hang on to these tight."

Doubtfully the old man clasped the electrodes. "This ain't going to hurt, is it, Doc?"

"It's just a kind of electrical bath," Sam soothed. "An electrical invigorator, you could say."

Cletus' Adam's-apple bobbed up and down.

"Ready?"

"I'm ready—I guess."

Sam twisted the handle, keeping his eye on the Electrical Charge Meter. Ten, twenty, thirty, forty—the instrument climbed slowly upscale. "I think," he mused, "that fifty is enough for now. At least, Dr. Perkins says that's suitable for mild cases of things." He looked up. "How does that feel?"

The old man had a glazed look. His hands, attached to the polished electrodes as if glued, trembled. The thicket of whiskers stood out, bristled.

"Cletus!" Sam dropped the crank and ran to him. "Are you all right? This is the first time I tried it out and—Cletus, talk to me! Say something!"

The old man swayed to his feet, eyes wide and staring. He clawed at his beard, stared around the disordered room. "Lordamighty!" Sam put an arm under his elbow to support the tottering figure, but Cletus pushed him away. "Jesus Christ and all the

Apostles! Why, I'm a-seein' stars all over my head! I ain't had a feeling like that since I put down a quart of forty-rod whisky on a dare!"

"Here!" Sam begged, contrite. "Sit down on this chair and rest! I think the Electrical Charge was too much for your system!"

Cletus refused the proffered chair. "Wait a minute," he said thoughtfully. "Wait just a minute!" He licked his lips, shook like a ragged spaniel emerging from the water, blinked bloodshot eyes. "I feel kind of all jingled up inside, Doc! You know, it ain't a half-bad feeling!" He took a few tentative steps, tottered, regained his feet.

"Sit down!" Sam implored. "There may be aftereffects!"

Cletus pushed his hand aside. "I kind of feel all tightened up inside," he grinned. "Full of the devil, too!" He shoved the battered felt hat rakishly over one eye and picked up his warbag. "Why, that machine's a wonder! Made me feel like a new man! Think I'll sashay over to Bertha's place and tell her all about it!"

"Cletus!" Sam called. "Come back here!" But Cletus did not heed his call. Frisking down Water Street, he greeted everyone he met, full of good spirits and the milk of human kindness. The last Sam saw of him he was climbing the rickety steps of Bertha's place, the last bordello remaining in Fitch's Landing. Sam cursed the urge that, at Pea Ridge or Cold Harbor or wherever it was during the war, had persuaded him to take up mending bodies instead of maiming them.

Afterward, he sat for a long time in the gloom of the office. The weather had changed, as it often did, quickly. A light snow was falling and the skies were gray. On a tin plate lay the remains of a slab of Ma Bidwell's raisin pie, half eaten. Soon heavy winter drifts would lie on the valley of the Yellowstone. Already early snows had mantled the peaks of the Chetish and the Big Horns. He would have to make a decision quickly. Stay, or go?

Finally he slept, a troubled sleep, and when he woke it was full dark. He would have to have a talk with Clara first, of course. He sewed up a rent in the sleeve of his long black coat, shaved, and rubbed grease into his scuffed boots. Slicking down his unruly black hair, he walked down River Street to the small frame house where Clara and her widowed mother lived. Clara taught school, and Mrs. Freeman baked pies and cakes for the soldiers at Fort Pike; somehow they managed to get along, though life was hard for them after Mr. Freeman died and they had moved into town.

"Why, Sam!" Mrs. Freeman exclaimed. "Come in! Clara and I were just talking about you!"

"Ma'am," he said, taking off his hat and scraping boots on the stoop. Clara sat by the stove grading papers. She looked up and smiled.

"Now I've just put by some bread to raise," Mrs. Freeman said, bustling about. She liked Sam Blair and did not care too much for Andy Wyatt with his airs and his expensive horses. "You and Clara set awhile and talk."

He sat opposite her, stiffly, on the edge of the rosewood chair the Freemans had brought from Iowa before Clara's father died of the lung fever.

"Your ma," he said. "She looks well."

Clara nodded. "She cries at night sometimes, but she's getting over it. She and Papa were so close."

He cleared his throat. "Ah—Clara."

She looked up from the papers she was examining.

"I—I want to talk to you. About—us."

She laid down the pencil, folded hands in her lap. Her blond hair, combed tightly back, glowed like fine gold in the lamplight.

"I guess you know the doctor business isn't so good here. I came out to the Territory with high hopes three years ago—going to be a *real* doctor, on the frontier where people needed me, not one of those fancy society doctors in St. Louis. But things didn't turn out right." Gloomily he stared into his hat. "Right now I've got a few dollars in cash; that's *all* I've got, except for my instruments and medical supplies, and most of that isn't paid for."

She looked questioningly at him, blue eyes dark pools in the glow of the Argand lamp.

"You and me," he went on, "we had an understanding. But Clara —I can't support a wife out here. Now I thought if you could see your way clear to come back with me to Springfield, Illinois— that's where my folks are—why, I've got credit at the bank there, and a lot of friends. Maybe we could make a go of it together. You could bring your ma, and—"

Clara's voice was tense. "I couldn't do that, Sam!"

"But—"

"I—I'm very honored to have known you, Sam, and I think you're a fine man. Once—once I told you I loved you. I still do, you see—" She put a gentle hand on his, leaned forward in the lamplight. "But in a different way, now, I guess. Anyway"—she sat back, stared at the pencil in her slender fingers—"Andrew Wyatt has asked me to marry him."

"Andy Wyatt?"

She hurried on, anxious to forestall him. "I've grown to know and like Andy very much. Life out here is so dull, Sam, and Andy has told me so much about his home back east. He's lived in Boston and New York and Washington and knows all about society and fancy dress balls and how to dance the schottische and what rich folks serve at their banquets on Fifth Avenue—champagne and caviar and things like that. I—I think I'd like to taste champagne, and I know I'd like caviar. Anyway, Andy's soon to be promoted, and it's possible his next duty station will be at the War Department. They consider him a promising young officer, and he wants to take me there with him."

Seeing the misery in his eyes, her own dimmed with tears. "Sam, I never meant to hurt you! But Andy is offering me so much—so much more! Washington, the capitol! Big hotels and fancy dress balls at the Willard Hotel! They've even got a street railway there —no more walking in the mud! Gas lamps, Andy says, and concerts! I—I—" She broke off. Biting her lip, she bent over the stack of papers, pretending to arrange them. "I'm sorry! I didn't mean to go on so, Sam. It was rude of me." A tear splashed onto the topmost paper, spread into a pale blot.

"You're not rude, Clara," he sighed. "You're just telling the truth. Andy Wyatt is a young man with a promising career, and I couldn't offer you the half of what he can. You know—" he swallowed painfully—"you know I wish the two of you only the best." He rose, held out his hand, still stained with the black carbolate that wouldn't come off. "Good-by, then, Clara."

Trembling, she said, "Sam—wait—"

They stood, facing each other across the lampshine, neither speaking. After a while Sam made an awkward gesture of farewell and opened the door. The last he saw of Clara Freeman was the sight of her standing in the lampglow, unable to speak further as he had been unable.

When he got back to the office, Cletus Wiley was sitting there, whittling a stick. Sam pushed a rag into the broken window, put the last chunk of wood into the stove. It was getting cold.

"You look like nine miles of bad road," Cletus observed.

Sam sat down, stared absently at the orange flicker behind the slotted iron door of the stove. "I'm leaving town, Cletus."

"Leaving town?"

"Can't make a go of it here. Guess I'll go back to Springfield and start all over again."

The old man spat delicately at the iron bowl of the stove. The stain spread, bubbled, stank. "Clara Freeman going with you then?"

Sam shook his head. "She and I just had a little talk. Seems she and Andy Wyatt out at Fort Pike are making their own plans, and they don't include me."

Cletus resumed whittling. "Guess everyone in town knew it before you did, Doc." Peeling white curls from the stick of pine, he asked, "When you leavin'?"

"Nothing to keep me here any longer. I'll take Thelma and the trap and ride the old Military Road to Fort Buford. There's a stage from there to Yankton. Then I can take the Chicago and Northwestern home."

"You need any money?"

"I've got a little. At Bismarck I can probably sell Thelma and the trap for fifty dollars or so. I'll make out all right."

Cletus threw away the stick and rose to examine the Tractors in their red-plush-lined case. "You know," he mused, "I got a little dust put away for my old age. I'll give it all to you—a good six ounces, I'd say—for these here Magnetic Tractors."

"Whatever for?"

"Well," Cletus said, "you know when you furnished me that treatment?"

"Yes."

"I went over to Bertha Rambouillet's place and stayed all afternoon with Hermione—you know, the French gal with the frizzy curls all over her head? I ain't been able to do anything like that for a long time! When I go up this winter to see my Brulé squaw on the Musselshell, I'd admire to take these along to kind of refresh myself from time to time."

Sam shook his head. "Those are *medical* instruments, Cletus. It'd be against my Hippocratic oath to put them in the hands of anyone that wasn't a doctor."

Cletus was disappointed, but stayed to help Sam pack his few belongings.

"What in hell you goin' to do with all this stuff?" he asked, pointing to the baskets of potatoes, pears, apples, the drowsy chickens in their crates.

"Take it over to Ma Bidwell's when I'm gone. She's carried me on credit for a long time. Maybe this will help pay for her kindness."

In the morning he didn't want to see Ma Bidwell or anyone else. After all his grandiose plans, he was sneaking out of town. In a cold and frosty dawn he hitched up old Thelma and stowed his personal effects and medical instruments and supplies into the space back of the seat, lashing a canvas over them. While he was packing, Cletus came in, nose red from the cold, beating chilblained hands together.

"You ain't had no breakfast yet, Doc. Ain't a good idea to go on a long trip without something in your stomach. Want me to have Ma Bidwell fry you up some eggs?"

"I'm not hungry," Sam said. He shook hands. "You've been a good friend, Cletus. I'm grateful."

The old man fidgeted nervously, spat a brown bull's-eye into the snow. "Fitch's Landing won't never be the same without you, Doc. You was a scholar and a gentleman, and there ain't many of your kind in the Territory. You sure you want to leave?"

"I'm sure," Sam said. "It's final, Cletus."

If he had thought to go away unseen, he was mistaken. As the trap wheeled round the corner and into River Street, he was confronted by a crowd. Ma Bidwell was there, wrapped in a shawl; Joe Harris, who ran the general store and whose shingles Sam had cured; Bertha Rambouillet and her girls, red-eyed and yawning from rising so early; Charlie Daigle, proprietor of the livery stable, whose broken arm Sam had set; and even Jake Almayer, father of the new daughter Sam had brought into the world, had ridden all the way into town. Ma Bidwell held up a magisterial hand.

"Wait a minute, Doc! We got a little talkin' to do!"

There was a chorus of agreement.

"We know your circumstances, and we found out you intend to leave town. You're as poor as the rest of us, but you never let that interfere with treatin' our fevers and busted legs and birthing our kids."

"That's right!" someone called.

Ma held up a chamois bag. "Since the Landing went to pot, most of us is lucky to get three squares a day and a roof over our heads, wood for the stove, a shirt for our backs. There ain't but precious little money around, but we scratched and scraped and took up a collection to help you pay your debts and maybe persuade you to stay amongst us a little longer."

Nonplussed, Sam turned to Cletus Wiley. "Is this shivaree your idea?"

The old man looked injured. "Doc, everyone in the Landing knows you ain't got any money! Besides, look at it this way—it ain't no more than the rightful amounts that's due you anyway for all the doctorin' you done free gratis around here!"

"That's right!" Jake Almayer called. "There's a dollar of mine in that bag, and soon's my crop comes in I'll pay off the rest!"

Touched, Sam shook his head.

"Folks, I can't do it. I can't take the money. God knows times are hard on the Yellowstone. What with winter coming on, you all need every cent you can lay your hands on. But I'm sure honored to think you like me enough to—to—" He blinked and had to turn his head away.

"Wisht you would," Ma said. "Out here in the Territory we was gettin' used to sickness and injury and dyin'—that's just the way things *was*, seems. Then you come along, a real doctor. So if you could see your way clear, Doc—"

"I'm sorry," Sam muttered. "I—I just can't do it. It wouldn't be right to saddle all of you with my problems. So I'll just say good-by and be grateful I knew you people. You're the salt of the earth."

Ma Bidwell spoke to her young son Mark, and he ran across the
street and returned with a bag of fresh crullers and a towel-
wrapped bottle of hot coffee for Sam Blair. "Anyway," she said,
blowing her nose, "our thoughts go with you, Doc. Write us when
you get back to Illinois or wherever it is."

Cletus reached into his ever-present warbag and took out the old
Starr revolver again. "You got better 'n fifty miles to go," he pointed
out, "and there ain't anyplace to hole up in that stretch if some late-
wandering Sioux decides to lift your hair. Take this along—please,
Doc? I'd sleep better tonight if I knowed you had a weapon on that
Godforsook Military Road!"

Sam tried to laugh, but his emotions were too near the surface.
"All right," he agreed. "If you want me to. And thank you. But like
I said, that pistol is a bigger danger to me than it is to any Sioux!"

The dawn was a long stripe of orange in a gunmetal sky when he
and Thelma wheeled out of town. Ominous flakes of snow drifted
down. On a hill above Fitch's Landing he reined up, looked back.
The place had never been pretty, but good people lived there.

He had never been so cold. Huddled in the seat of the trap with
a blanket around him, shawl pulled over his hat and around his
ears, hands in heavy mittens, Sam began to doubt he should have
tried the trip. Yesterday it still seemed Indian summer. Today the
wind whistled and moaned through the trees, lifting the dusting of
snow into whorls and spirals. There was no sun, only Thelma's patient broad back and bobbing ears as he stared straight ahead,
wondering if his ears were freezing.

Weather in the Territory changed suddenly. It was risky to set off
alone in changeable weather. But that was the thing Sam first noticed out here. A man went ahead and did what he wanted without
let or hindrance. If he did not succeed—well, that was the Territory
for you.

The road was straight and narrow, marked every few miles by a
sagging wooden sign that said FORT BUFORD one way and FORT PIKE
the other, with appropriate arrows. For now, there was little chance
of losing his way.

At noon he stopped in the scanty shelter of a grove of leafless cottonwoods, gave Thelma a quart of oats in the nosebag, and ate the

crullers. In his mind he could see Clara Freeman's golden hair, blue eyes brimming with tears, the way she looked in the lamplight when he closed the door on his love. A diffident and reserved man, Sam Blair never cut much of a figure with the ladies. It was as much as his deaf-mute parents could do merely to keep him at the Academy, their scanty savings eked out by his own clerking at the grocery store. When there were socials in Springfield, or a Friday night "musical" at the Academy, he generally had to work late. He had never had a social life worthy of the name, and lacked the easy graces he admired in others—like Andy Wyatt.

"Clara!" he sighed, so loud old Thelma perked up her ears and looked around at him.

As he resumed the journey there was a faint silvery glow in the clouds overhead. It might be the truant sun, but the day continued cold and windy. To add to his problems, Thelma started to act up. Suddenly the old mare would pull up, whinny, and start a clumsy caracole, as if she saw a rattlesnake in the barren road. But there were no snakes out in this weather. Puzzled, Sam reined up and climbed down to rub her gray muzzle.

"Come on, girl!" he said patiently. "Only another twenty miles or so. Then it's a nice warm stall for you, and flapjacks and coffee for me."

Thelma continued to act oddly. It was almost as if she were trying to tell him something. Again he dismounted, examining her hoofs, thinking perhaps she had bruised a frog on a stone. But the hoofs were all sound.

When she persisted in the strange behavior, he became exasperated. Stopping up near a copse of frozen willows bordering the Military Road, he held her halter for a while, trying to reason with her. She rolled her eyes and jerked at the halter.

"Not much farther now," he insisted. He squinted at the sun, emerging from a wraith of clouds. "There, see that? That's a good sign, Thelma! Now let's stop this silly dancing around and get on, shall we?"

He was standing there, talking to the frightened mare, when out of the willows galloped the Sioux. They were a dozen or more, wrapped in blankets and carrying modern-looking rifles. Some wore fur hats, others were bareheaded. Quickly they surrounded him and his buggy, kneeing their ponies close so he could hardly move. He felt the hot steamy whuffling of the paint ponies in his face. Now he knew what Thelma had been trying to tell him.

CHAPTER 2

"*Haul*" Sam quavered. Cletus Wiley had told him that was the way to address a Sioux. It meant, "Hello, friend!"

These did not look like friends. They were big men, broad-shouldered, faces painted. They stared at him with curiosity, surprised as he was.

"Haul" he said again, and held up his hand, palm open. The Starr revolver was in the valise behind the seat. But even if he had it to hand, what good would it do against seasoned Indian warriors?

"I—I was just going to Fort Buford," he said conversationally, trying to keep his voice from trembling. "That way." He pointed. Did any of them understand English? "I don't mean anyone any harm. I'm a doctor—a physician, you see."

What were they doing along the Military Road so late in the season? By this time they were supposed to be in their winter camps. Chilled and uncertain, Sam finally said, "Well, I've got to be going now. Fort Buford is a long way. If you'll just stand aside—"

Things happened after that so quickly, so murderously, that he was rooted to the spot. One of the band cut the reins and dragged poor old Thelma, bleating like a calf, to the side of the road. When Sam tried to intervene someone jumped on him, knocking him sprawling, and bound his hands and feet. A brave in a tattered blue military overcoat with tarnished brass buttons slashed Thelma's throat and stepped back, grinning. The old mare trembled, kicked once or twice, and died, stiff-legged.

Like a band of gleeful children the Oglalas ransacked the trap, throwing out blankets, clothing, books, tearing open bundles and boxes. They appeared entranced by his medical kit. A pockmarked man opened all his bottles of pills, tasted the ipecac, stared wonderingly at the shiny electrodes of the Magnetic Tractors. Dragging the device by its long cords, he jumped down off the trap and came to where Sam lay bound. He looked at Sam, and then back at the Tractors.

"You—fix people?" he inquired in a hoarse voice.

They were the first words of English Sam had heard in this brutal encounter, and they gave him a surge of hope. Men who spoke English, even such imperfect English, could not be utter brutes.

"Yes," he admitted. "I'm a doctor, a physician."

Pockmark wound the electrical cords of the Tractors into a skein. "You—you fix broken—" He sought for words. Finally he held up a hand. "Bad hand?"

Sam nodded. "I'm a surgeon. Yes, I can fix injured limbs."

"Limms?"

Sam indicated his hands, feet. "Fix," he said.

Many injuries were beyond his capability—beyond any surgeon's capabilities—but he saw no need to go into details in a dangerous situation.

Pursing his lips, Pockmark walked away, dangling the skein of electrical wire. Putting the Tractors back in their box, he also replaced the scattered vials and bottles. He appeared to be in some authority; when one brave did not want to relinquish Sam's bone saw, Pockmark barked something curt and the man handed it meekly over.

Their fun finished, the Oglalas chopped seasoned oak from Sam's trap with their hatchets to make a small fire. They sat around it in their blankets, paying Sam no more attention than if he had been a bundle of cornstalks in a field. One of them carved bloody steaks from Thelma's haunch, and they stuck the meat on willow switches and roasted it. Sam had never seen men eat so much meat. They must have been out on a long scout and run low on provisions, he thought. They roasted chunk after chunk of horsemeat, took them out of the flames while they were still only half cooked, and stuffed themselves till faces and hands were smeared with blood and grease. All Sam could do was wriggle helplessly in his bonds, damn himself for a fool to undertake the ride through Oglala-infested country, and be grateful they had not slaughtered him the way they had dispatched poor old Thelma—at least, not yet.

As they ate, the Oglalas engaged in a long discussion. The pockmarked man did most of the talking. Some of the others argued in the choking, sibilant Sioux tongue, accompanied by a great deal of sign talk. Frequently the pockmarked man glanced over, jerked his thumb at Sam Blair, and then resumed his harangue.

Alert, he watched them, thinking he was beginning to understand some of the hand talk. Many of the gestures reminded him of the sign language his parents had used to communicate with their small son. Over the years Sam had become adept, even finding a kind of beauty in the fluttering hands, the quick fingers. The Oglalas were certainly talking about him, Sam Blair, but what were they saying?

Hunger sated, they ended their discourse. Rising, they patted their bellies, pulled their mounts to them. One man, grinning, offered Sam a chunk of half-raw horsemeat. It was too much for him; gagging, he bent over. They laughed, and a man with Sam's Starr revolver in his belt tied Sam's feet together under the belly of a lead horse. Before they left, they gathered up the remains of the trap and hid it in the willows, along with the remains of poor Thelma. The extra meat they wrapped in an old canvas and strapped to a packhorse. Packing Sam's medical kit also, they left the Military Road, turning off at a diagonal and striking off across the snow-dusted valley toward the great escarpment of the Chetish.

On the trail they did not pay Sam a great deal of attention, though when the pockmarked man saw him shivering, he took an extra blanket from a bundle and threw it over Sam's shoulders. The gesture was quick and impersonal, almost as if Sam were a prize steer to be protected until made into steaks.

In late afternoon the sun emerged, painting the broad bulk of the mountains with splashes of gold, sparkling and luminous where lay patches of early snow. The little party toiled up a long slope toward the draws that slashed the flanks of the Chetish. Dazed and disoriented, Sam stared at the fantastic gorges and canyons. Was there a trail that way? Surely no one could find a path up that fissured slope. But the Sioux bore steadily on. When dusk came, they made camp in a tangle of stunted oaks as if they had known all along they were bound for that spot.

They had brought some of the horsemeat with them, and they started another fire and ate again. Angrily Sam refused a roasted chunk of what would have been sirloin, he guessed, on a steer.

After tying Sam up the Sioux slept, lying around the fire wrapped in blankets. From time to time one rose to make water, casually inspected the prisoner's bonds, and slept again. When his own bladder was full, Sam managed to rouse the pockmarked brave. His late antagonist yawned, stretched, and got up, taking off Sam's bonds. Then he tied his prisoner tightly again and went back to sleep beside the dying fire.

Drifting across the night, an owl hooted. A rind of moon was caught in the tangle of limbs over Sam's head, and he was very cold. He had a feeling of unreality. For a moment everything seemed to rock and sway under him, the earth heaving and twisting and rolling. Then, in spite of the chill, he broke out in a sweat and knew it was nerves. *Clara,* he thought miserably, *Clara, you would be sorry for me now!*

It was not yet dawn when they started off again. These men knew the trail so well they simply rode into the blackness. It was a good hour before the eastern sky was lit with pale color. Up, up, and yet up they rode, so that now the trees were gone; all that remained were clumps of stunted juniper and bare rock. Unshod hoofs slipping and sliding in frosted shale, the ponies struggled onward, breath puffing out in clouds of vapor. At last, near the summit, morning sun emerged from a rack of clouds. The band halted, mounts exhausted, all grateful for the sunlight.

They were atop the Chetish, the range white men called the Wolf Mountains. Far below them lay the valley, river winding sinuously through the trees and glinting in spots with a sheen of new ice. Around them snow-mantled peaks reared massive abutments. The air was thin and cold, but bracing. Some of the Sioux dismounted and squatted, chanting a kind of litany to the sun—one of their gods, Sam supposed. Others stretched and yawned, chatting among themselves.

"Where are you taking me?" Sam croaked, but got no answer.

For the first time, he managed to collect his thoughts enough to take stock of the curious situation. They had not killed him. And his medical kit was packed carefully on one of the horses, lashed in place. What value was he, or the kit, to them?

That night the mood of the men subtly changed. They talked a lot, sang in a high-pitched sort of chorale, joked frequently with each other. Even after the moon rose they kept on, riding down now through thick groves of pine and fir. The branches were heavily laden with snow, but the pine-needle floor was soft and fragrant and resilient. At what must have been midnight they rode into their camp, a moonlit cup of valley studded with dozens of lodges, each glowing like a giant taper from the fire within.

People streamed from the lodges, the open doorflaps fire-lit. They came to greet the returning warriors, calling out and laughing. The stolid faces of Sam's captors relaxed; they slid down from their ponies and told stories of their adventures. Pockmark made a great deal of Sam Blair, and a crowd of the curious thronged about the prisoner as he sat bound and silent on his horse. They pulled at his clothing, nudged him, made remarks. One of the children wrenched at his boot and tore it off, running giggling into the night.

After a while, tired, the men of the returning band thrust him, still bound, into a shabby smoke-stained lodge at the edge of a circle of tipis. A guard was posted to watch, and the camp settled into silence.

Lying in the Sioux lodge, helpless to move, Sam felt the true dimension of his fear. The attack on the Military Road, the slaughter of old Thelma and the burning of his trap, the long ride to the summit of the Chetish and down into the hostile camp—all these had been motion and violence and quick-changing circumstance, leaving him dazed and confused. Now, however, he lay cold and sweating in the blackness, brain completely clear—too clear—weighing one thing against the other, this against that, calculating, guessing, hoping, despairing. Why had they not killed him, quickly and cleanly, the way they had poor old Thelma? Why had they troubled to bring him all this way?

He thought of Stone's Landing, during the war, and a man the cavalry vedettes caught whom they said was a Rebel spy. The vedettes had bound that man, too, and thrust him into a tent, with a guard. In a red-streaked morning, they took him out and hanged him to an elm tree. *But I'm not a spy,* he thought. *I'm just a curiosity to them—something to amuse, like a bug in a bottle.* After they tired of playing with him, as a cat plays with a mouse, they would kill him; not hang him—that was the civilized way to do it—but torture him, put flaming splinters under his nails, mutilate him.

After a while the burden of thought became too much; he slept. In the middle of the night, he woke, hearing the faraway yipping of a band of coyotes. Moonlight streaked the thin-scraped hide walls of the ancient lodge. He slept fitfully, and when he awoke it was morning.

The pockmarked man came to the lodge and undid his bonds. Struggling up, Sam swayed for a moment on feet that seemed blocks of wood, without feeling or relevance. Rubbing chafed wrists, feeling reviving blood tingle into his hands, he asked, "What's going to happen to me?"

The man only pushed him out of the lodge, pointing toward the big tipi in the middle of the frosted meadow.

"Where are you taking me?" Sam insisted.

Pockmark gestured again toward the lodge.

"All right," Sam grumbled. "I'm going." Hobbling on a bootless and half-frozen foot, he stumbled on.

The Sioux encampment was large. Through sleep-bleared eyes he saw what must be over a hundred lodges and a brush corral teeming with ponies. Smoke curled from cooking fires, then lay flat to drift horizontally as if some natural ceiling existed. Morning sun was bright on sticklike figures painted on the lodges—crude yet lively depictions of men and horses, with large serrated suns and zigzag designs like strokes of lightning. Children played in the meadow, and an old man sat in a doorway painstakingly cutting a trade skillet into arrowheads. It was a town of sorts; nothing like Springfield, Illinois, nor yet Fitch's Landing, I. T., yet oddly similar. Hobbling alone with one boot, Sam wondered what the morning was going to bring.

At the doorflap of the great lodge lounged a group of men, like courtiers at the antechamber of a great king. They wore winter clothing; buffalo-skin moccasins with high tops, leggings of dark woolen cloth, buckskin shirts with the hair outside. Some sported trailing gee strings of red flannel, and all were wrapped in fine trade blankets. One man's face was painted with an intricate design of white dots. Another had a fur hat with a stuffed yellowhammer on top. A third was bare-chested, the skin of his breast pitted with deep scars; he wore his blanket loosely kilted around the waist, held in place by a cartridge belt. They were a hard-bitten and competent-looking lot, reminding Sam Blair of the veterans of the Sixteenth Illinois when they came home from the war to march down Pennsylvania Avenue. Insolently they stared, made comments, grinned, until the pockmarked man shoved him through the doorflap and into the smoky interior of the great lodge.

Previously dazzled by the sunlit meadow, he could not see in the dimness of the lodge. Then, as his vision sharpened, he found himself at the periphery of a vast circle, perhaps thirty feet or more in diameter. In the center smoldered a fire. Ranged around its red eye sat a council, probably the elders of the tribe. On a rude throne, an ammunition box partially covered with a buffalo robe, squatted an old man. Though his face was crazed with thousands of wrinkles like a glass dish brought too near the fire, there was a kingly presence to him. The gray hair was dressed in braids and a single eagle feather stuck straight up from his topknot. In spite of his apparent age, the shoulders and neck were powerful and muscular, though one hand appeared wizened and useless.

"Hau!" Sam ventured, rubbing chafed wrists.

There was only a faint pop from the fire, obsidian-hard eyes. Judging from the stony silence, he had broken a protocol. But Pockmark quickly took over the ceremonies. Spreading Sam's medical kit on the hard-packed earth—surgical instruments, pill bottles, stethoscope, the Magnetic Tractors, everything—he launched into a long speech, with much gesticulating.

Beside the chief—it must be Left Hand himself—stood an imposing figure. The face was cruel: nose hooked, thin lips compressed into a slit, eyes deep-set and calculating. The Oglala, who appeared to be a shaman, wore blue paint on his face, with a white moon on the forehead and a star across the bridge of the beaklike nose. On his head was a band of black fur with a buffalo horn attached to each ear. Impatiently he twitched a switch made from a buffalo tail fastened to a short stick.

When Pockmark paused for a moment, pointing with pride to his prisoner and the array of medical gear, Sam seized the opportunity. "You can't do this!" he protested. "Pretty quick the Army will notice I've disappeared, and they'll come after me!"

The remark was inane, and the Oglalas disregarded it.

Pockmark continued with his oration. From time to time he

picked up a bottle of cough syrup, a surgical saw, the stethoscope, displaying them. Buffalo Horns appeared to be bored with the whole business. Left Hand, chin propped on good hand, listened with interest.

Finally Pockmark finished his presentation. Even before he finished, Sam knew somehow what his captor had done. Then he realized that Pockmark used the same sign Sam's deaf-mute parents employed—a quick brushing of one palm across the other. *Finished, completed, the end.*

Buffalo Horns spat, started to speak. But Left Hand gestured and the shaman fell silent. Slowly, regally, the chief rose, wrapping a blanket about his furrowed middle. Stepping down from the dais, he examined the litter of medical supplies. In addition to the withered hand, the chief's right leg appeared also to be thin and unsubstantial; probably, Sam thought, the result of a childhood disease. Such things affected Sioux Indians as well as white children. Many times Sam had attempted to treat the sickness, but without success. Generally it started with fever, joint and muscular pains. Sometimes it resulted in death, from paralysis of the chest muscles. When a child recovered, it was usually as a cripple, with weak and atrophied arms and legs.

When Left Hand pointed, Pockmark was quick to hand up the items. The chief shook powdered alum into a leathery palm, tasted, spat it out in disgust. "Wagh!" He tried a swig of the Special Catarrhal Remedy Sam himself had compounded and then tossed the bottle away, making a face.

"Well," Sam muttered, "it cures the catarrh, no matter what you say!"

Finally Left Hand motioned toward the Magnetic Tractors. Pockmark snatched them up and handed them over. Firelight glanced from the polished surfaces, darted in jewel-like beams on the smoke-stained skins of the lodge. For a moment the chief seemed interested. He rubbed a hand over the metal, reeled in a few feet of the dangling electrical cords. He frowned, puzzled, at the blank face of the Electrical Charge meter. Buffalo Horns watched, buffalo-tail switch twitching in boredom. Again the shaman started to speak, but Left Hand ignored him. Turning to Sam, he spoke in heavily accented English.

"You docker?"

Pockmark too had spoken some English. Sam supposed they had picked it up at treaty talks, or from trading with the white men before the present troubles.

He nodded. "Yes. I am a doctor."

Left Hand held up the withered hand. The tendons had drawn up so that the leathery claw was bent almost back on itself.

"You fix—this?"

The crippled hand trembled as Left Hand held it near Sam's face. Left Hand's dark eyes stared into his.

"You fix?" The chief repeated.

There was silence in the smoky lodge. Buffalo Horns stared at Sam, Left Hand scanned his face, the council of elders smoked quietly, watching. Pockmark patted Sam on the back in an encouraging gesture.

"That hand?" Sam asked. "Your—your hand?"

Left Hand said nothing; watched him, intent.

Sam shook his head. "No, I can't fix."

Perhaps they did not understand the words, but the spectators read the look on the old man's face. There was a collective sigh. Pockmark was chagrined, but Buffalo Horns grinned.

Stung, Sam cried out, "Well, I bet you can't do any better, even with those silly buffalo horns on your head!"

Left Hand nudged the litter on the ground with a moccasined toe. "These your medicine, eh?"

They were indeed Sam's medicines, along with a lot of other medical adjuncts. But he understood what Left Hand meant. To a Sioux, medicine signified sacred objects, magic things—charms, talismen, supernatural influences. Old Cletus Wiley carried a small buckskin bag around his neck containing yellowhammer feathers, pebbles with flecks of gold, a dry and rustling snakeskin; *his* medicine, Cletus explained, given for protection by his Brulé woman.

"Yes," Sam acknowledged. "Medicine. White man's medicine."

Buffalo Horns grinned scornfully. Pointing the buffalo-tail switch at Sam, he guffawed. The elders joined in mocking chorus.

"But—no fix this?" Left Hand held up the withered hand.

Regretfully, Sam shook his head again. As a physician he would

truly like to have helped the old man, regardless of his personal
danger in the Oglala camp.

Jumping from the dais, Buffalo Horns prowled menacingly toward Sam, jabbing with the switch, growling like an angry bear. He
kicked aside the bottles, powders, the amputation saw, the scalpel.
Jeering, he pranced about.

"But you don't understand!" Sam cried. "A doctor can't cure *everything!* Anyway, we can do a lot of good, if we're let!" He
scrabbled in the litter, held up a bottle. "Laudanum, for the intrac-
table pain of gout!" He found more bottles. "Quinine for the ma-
laria, Blaud's pills for anemia! I can cure the dropsies, scrofula, female diseases!" Snatching up the patent stethoscope, he dangled it
in Buffalo Horns' face. "I can listen to peoples' insides with this instrument—tell if they've got congestion of the lungs, whether the
heart needs an infusion of foxglove!"

Behind him, Pockmark made encouraging sounds.

"But I can't fix that hand!" Sam admitted. "It's beyond modern
surgery, and that's a fact!"

Buffalo Horns sneered, seeing a rival defeated. Arrogant, he
stalked to the firelit circle, reaching into a leather pouch slung on a
strap beneath his arm. Left Hand, wrapped in his blanket, watched,
face impassive.

Taking a handful of something from the pouch, Buffalo Horns
strutted around the fire, chanting in high-pitched singsong. As he
circled he performed an intricate shuffling step, bending low, then
thrusting the garishly painted face high toward the open smoke flap
of the tipi.

"You're not such a much!" Sam murmured. "You're a quack, a
damned quack, that's all!"

Buffalo Horns began to howl, a high-pitched keening. Fascinated,
the elders watched him. Suddenly his voice changed. Mimicking a
bird, arms outspread, he whistled in deep liquid tones. The council
watched. Left Hand watched. Pockmark watched, also, but was not
impressed; his lip curled. Pockmark and Buffalo Horns, Sam suspected, were not good friends.

Faster and faster Buffalo Horns danced. He began to screech. To
Sam Blair it sounded like a catamount he had once come upon near

Jake Almayer's place. Watching intently also, Sam was unnerved to find himself becoming unaccountably faint. Was it a kind of hypnotic spell? Or was the reaction from the violent events of the days before beginning to catch up with him? Passing a hand across his forehead, it came away cold and sweaty. Indian medicine, Sioux medicine—Was Buffalo Horns doing something to him?

One of the spectators picked up a drum, a simple affair of painted skin stretched tight across a wooden hoop, and began to thump. The tempo matched the acceleration of Sam Blair's own pulse, thudding heavily in his temples. Feeling giddy, he bit his lip hard, pain bringing him back to reality.

"Ow—ee—ee!" Buffalo Horns screamed. Suddenly he cast a yellowish powder into the fire. It flared in a great whoosh, sending up a cloud of sparks, a gush of white smoke. The smoke behaved curiously; it boiled and bubbled, twisted and writhed. To Sam's astonished eyes it took form—the form of an animal of some kind. A deer? Was it a deer? Dazed he peered at the rolling vapors. A bear, a great bear rearing upright? Perhaps a gigantic bird, a prehistoric monster?

Sinuously the smoke twined about, drawing in and out of itself in complicated coils. Was that a *snake?* Sam rubbed bleary eyes.

"Oweeeeeee!" Buffalo Horns screeched again and disappeared in the clouds of smoke. *A drug.* Sam thought. *A drug of some sort— the powder Buffalo Horns had thrown into the fire must be a powerful drug.*

When the pulsing drum stopped, the smoke cleared, Buffalo Horns, sweating and exhausted, stood again at the side of Left Hand. With a wave of his buffalo-tail switch, he acknowledged the grunted approvals of the elders. This was medicine, *real* medicine, his triumphant face proclaimed.

For two days Sam had little sleep and less food. He knew the tricks a weakened brain could play. It had all been an illusion compounded by his own confused thoughts and a hypnotic drug. The Great Kellerman, on tour through Springfield, had done much the same thing and did not need drugs. But the performance did make Sam Blair's medicine look puny.

Left Hand apparently thought so too. For a long time he stared at Sam, pulling his lower lip between thumb and forefinger, painted brow wrinkled in thought. At last he shrugged, almost regretfully, and made a gesture. *Finished. We are no longer amused. Take him away!*

"No!" Sam protested. "Wait a minute!"

Pockmark, embarrassed by Sam's failure, seized his arm to drag him from the lodge. Kicking like a steer, Sam resisted. Pockmark lost his grasp and Sam fell to the pounded earth, scrabbling in the litter of his medical kit. What did he have to lose? His practice was gone, his best girl was married to another man, he was a failure. Besides, though a patient and long-suffering man, he was becoming angry.

"I'll show you magic!" he yelled. Pushing Pockmark away he held up the Tractors. "You haven't seen any real magic till you've seen Dr. Perkins' Magnetic Tractors!"

They stared at him, thinking him taken with a fit.

"Will you take a dare?" He raised the Tractors high, long wires dangling snakelike. "I'll show you magic—white man's medicine!"

Seizing the initiative, he worked fast. He had to, or it was all over; *he* was all over; Sam Blair was all over. "You!" he called to Buffalo Horns. "Come over here!"

The shaman scowled, made an obscene gesture with thumb poked between first and second fingers.

"Come on!" Sam challenged. "You're such a big muckamuck—come here and try on white man's medicine!"

The lodge was silent. The old men stared at Sam, then at Buffalo Horns. The shaman seemed uneasy.

"I dare you!" Sam cried. "Come here!"

Left Hand made an almost imperceptible gesture. Unwillingly, Buffalo Horns laid down the fly switch, sidled near Sam.

"Right here," Sam said, crooking a finger. "Stand here, now. And take these electrodes—one in each hand, so!"

Buffalo Horns rolled his eyes like a skittish gelding. He clasped hands reluctantly around the metal tubes.

"Now!" Sam said. "You just stand there, like that, while I get ready to practice a little medicine!"

Intrigued, the old men signed to each other, muttered behind their hands. Left Hand sat regally on the improvised dais, watching. Pockmark hovered nearby, uncertain.

Squatting, Sam fumbled for the dynamo, got the wooden crank in his fingers. "Don't move!" he cautioned, like a photographer who has finally got a nervous subject to stand still. Satisfied, he gave the wooden handle a mighty spin.

Buffalo Horns trembled, seemed to vibrate. His mouth opened dumbly, the tongue lolling as if he were trying to speak. Under sagging lids his eyes rolled whitely upward. Trying to escape the spell, he took a shuffling step backward. The shaman's eyes were glassy; his teeth chattered. He tottered drunkenly about, unable to drop the metal tubes. Writhing, he opened his mouth wide and no sound emerged.

"No tricks!" Sam jeered. "No mumbo jumbo, no smoke to hide the ropes and pulleys and machinery! This is the real thing, friend!"

The needle of the indicating meter climbed far upscale, into the area marked DANGER—FOR CATTLE AND LARGE ANIMALS ONLY! For a moment Sam was afraid he smelled burning flesh. Relenting, he stopped cranking.

"Aaagh!" Buffalo Horns at last found his voice. Shaking paralyzed hands, he sprawled on the dirt floor.

"There!" Sam said triumphantly. "How's that?"

Left Hand pondered the thunderbolt that had struck his chief adviser. Taking out a carved scratching stick, he poked it into his topknot, working it thoughtfully back and forth. Eye to eye, Sam and the Oglala chief regarded each other. Finally the silence was broken by a giggle. Sam turned. Pockmark, putting a hand over his mouth, was not successful in stifling his amusement. He pointed to Buffalo Horns, lying loose-jointed like a rag doll on the beaten ground. Buffalo Horns groaned. His head rolled from side to side. Trying to get up, rubbery legs collapsed under him.

Sam pointed too. "Have you got anything to match that?" he cried. "A fresh batch of lightning bolts called down from the sky and bound to do my bidding! Medicine? I've got the real copper-riveted two-ply triple-distilled article!"

Left Hand did not join in the merriment. When one of the elders grinned, he stared somberly at the man and the grin faded. Pockmark, too, became quickly solemn. Drawing close, he whispered into Left Hand's ear, gesticulating. Seeming to ponder, Left Hand rubbed his chin. He watched Buffalo Horns, who at last had managed to struggle to his feet and blink owlishly about, still dazed. Finally Left Hand nodded. Pockmark, with an almost courtly gesture, indicated to Sam the audience was at an end. Sam was to follow him.

He did not know where they were going to take him or what they intended to do with him. But in a camp of bloodthirsty savages he was still alive and gave great credit to Dr. Perkins' Magnetic Tractors. Seizing them, he crammed them into his black satchel, along with the scattered bottles and instruments. "Goodby," he said over his shoulder and followed Pockmark out.

The Oglalas gave him his own tipi at the edge of the great village, returned his missing boot, brought him food. Pockmark bade him farewell, patting his shoulder.

"What's going to happen to me?" Sam asked.

Pockmark only grinned and walked out into the dusk.

That night Sam slept an almost drugged sleep. Waking before dawn, he felt a call of nature and limped into the icy night. Spraddle-legged in the snow, he stared at the star-studded heavens. *Clara!* he thought. *If you only could know where I am, the dangers I face*—But that was no good. His lost love slept peacefully under the same star-sprinkled canopy and could never know his travail. He felt alone, abandoned.

Then he noticed the guard. Rifle across his knees, a blanket-wrapped brave huddled near the doorway of the tipi, watching him. Left Hand's Oglalas, he realized, had not yet made up their minds what kind of a being Sam Blair was. And whatever happened, he had certainly made an enemy of old Buffalo Horns, the shaman.

CHAPTER 3

He was in limbo, an Indian limbo. Lying on a slatted mat of willow rods stitched with sinew, he lay in the tipi, listening to a rustle of icy particles as sleet fell on the smoke-blackened skins. He could hardly believe his situation: a white man, an inoffensive person who lived a humdrum life and had never known memorable happenings—this man suddenly in danger of his life, rudely transported to a Sioux camp, confined under guard in a swarm of red savages. It boggled the imagination.

His mind turned to home—to Springfield, to the Academy, to his parents. The thought acted as a comforting counterpoise to present peril. But would he ever see Springfield again, the silent parents, Indian summer with small boys wading knee-deep in leaves? Early frost on pumpkins, smoke curling from civilized hearthsides? Then, angry with himself for slipping into such maudlin thoughts, he drove one fist into the other and resolved to prevail. Like a sheep he had given Clara Freeman up to Andy Wyatt; now the game was life itself. This time he determined to prevail.

Days passed—one day, two days, three days—he lost track. The guard allowed him to leave the tent for only brief intervals. On these short excursions Sam wondered where everyone was. But the camp appeared deserted, almost lost to view in the downpour of snow. It drifted high around the lodges, lay heavy on the branches of the trees, mounded on the backs of ponies in the corral. Only a few wisps of smoke from the apexes of the lodges betrayed habitation. Lonely, he went back into the lodge, wishing he had a pencil and paper. He had always written a lot—childish stories when he was a boy, a diary at the Academy, long love letters to Clara which he labored over and then tore up. Now writing would help while away the solitude. But there was no paper, no pen—nothing but snow, and silence, and uncertainty.

After a week, or perhaps two, something did happen. Pockmark came diffidently into the lodge, squatted, lit his pipe from the small fire smoldering in the middle of the tipi. Sam remembered Cletus Wiley's stories about the Sioux. *A man does well never to speak first to a Sioux. If he comes to you and wants to palaver, just sit tight and let him bring up what's on his mind. It's etiket, see—like remembering not to fan hot soup with your hat when you're out in society.* So he squatted across the fire from Pockmark and said nothing. Finally Pockmark spoke.

"Me"—he slapped his bare chest, bare even in the dead of winter —"Growler." Rumbling deep in his throat, he rose on moccasined toes, making menacing motions with clawed hands, like a bear. "Growler," he repeated. "English name—Growler." He stared at Sam. "You name English?"

The hoarse voice did indeed sound like the coughing grunt of a bear that once invaded River Street in Fitch's Landing.

"Growler," Sam conceded. He slapped his own chest. "Sam."

"Sam?" Growler's brow furrowed. "Uh—Sam?"

"Yes, Sam."

Growler appeared to consider this name amusing. Grinning, he handed the pipe to Sam. "Smoke," he said. "Growler—Sam— friends."

In this desperate situation Sam was willing to have a friend of any kind. He accepted the pipe and took a deep drag. Not being a tobacco user himself, he immediately started to cough and wheeze. Growler's grin broadened. He retrieved the pipe from Sam and puffed again, clouds of smoke wreathing the pitted countenance.

"Friends," he repeated. "You—me."

"All right," Sam agreed. "That's good." What was Growler getting at?

"Friends—" Growler gestured toward Sam, then himself. "Friends help each."

"Each—other?"

Growler nodded. "Help each—other. Sam help Growler. Growler help Sam. Bring—" His brow furrowed, trying to think of a word. Finally he had it. "Present!" he exclaimed. "Bring present!" Putting fingers in his mouth, in exactly the way Sam Blair had done as a small boy in Springfield, he whistled shrilly. The doorflap opened, and a handsome young woman entered.

"Cook good," Growler advised him, nodding toward the female. "Name—" He reeled off words in the Sioux tongue, but in that strange hissing and choking Sam could make out nothing. Seeing Sam's perplexity, Growler stared at the open smoke flap, tongue lolling in thought. Apparently his English had failed. But finally the scarred countenance brightened. "Sweet," he said. He put fingers to his mouth. "Sweet—like—" Again he paused. "Sweet like honey."

Sam frowned. A lady named Sweet Honey?

Growler tried again. He made a sign Sam recognized as something growing from the ground.

"Grass?"

Growler nodded vigorously. "Sweet Grass!"

So she was named Sweet Grass! No, there was more! Growler raked fingers down his braids in a gesture resembling combing. It meant—it must mean—*woman*.

"Sweet Grass Woman!" Sam blurted.

Pleased, Growler slapped him on the back in that familiar gesture. "Sweet Grass Woman!"

Sam was not used to being with young females, even Sioux females, unchaperoned in a room; Mrs. Freeman had always been strict about that. Now, apparently, this Sioux female had been told off to do for him—cook, perhaps sweep out the lodge, maybe mend clothes—and what else? He was uneasy. Still, this was not exactly a room like the Freeman's parlor; it was a Sioux tipi. And it would certainly be discourteous to refuse a present.

"Thanks," he said, without conviction.

"You say—*hie, hie*," Growler instructed him.

Those words must be the Oglala equivalent of *thanks*.

"Hie, hie," he repeated, dutifully.

Growler rose, knocking the dottle from the pipe. "You—Sam," he said. He slapped his chest. "Growler."

"Yes," Sam agreed. "Thank you very much."

He went away, leaving Sam alone with the handsome young squaw.

Sam began to suspect Growler was a kind of politician in the Indian camp. Apparently he had brought Sam to Left Hand's camp in the hope of curing the chief's maimed hand, perhaps currying favor himself. Now that Sam had impressed the Oglalas with the Magnetic Tractors, perhaps Growler wanted to stand close to the electrical magic by favoring him with a woman. But the gift—the female present—was embarrassing.

Sweet Grass Woman stood near him. She was tall, almost as tall as he was, and lissome. Long braids shone sleek in the pale sun filtering through the skins of the lodge. Her breasts were full and round beneath the red cloth of the shirt. In her hand she held a round wooden bowl filled with bits of leathery dried meat and what appeared to be chokecherries.

"Eat?" she urged.

When she saw his confusion, she laughed. Taking out a bit of meat in her long brown fingers, she touched his lips gently with the food. "Eat," she urged.

Awkwardly Sam took the food in his own fingers, avoiding her amused glance. His hand trembled as he conveyed it to his mouth.

"Sweet—" he murmured. "Sweet Grass Woman! That's a pretty name."

She laughed again, innocently, and went to the doorflap to bring in a small child, a round-faced infant of two or three years, who scuttled crabwise on a twisted foot. Taking the tiny hand in her own, she thrust it at Sam's big paw.

The child, fearful, screamed in panic. Sweet Grass Woman sat down on a robe to comfort him. To add to Sam's uneasiness, she pulled aside the loose shirt and offered her breast. Reassured, the baby sucked happily while Sweet Grass Woman looked fondly down. The child, he realized, must be her own.

He stood at the doorflap, letting the cold wind bathe the forehead beaded with sudden perspiration. Whatever could he have been thinking of? This was an Indian woman, a *squaw!* Too, she might be diseased. Besides, she was married—or however Indians solemnized the union of man and wife!

With the quickness common in the Territory, the weather changed again. As Sam languished in captivity the snow ceased, the drifts started to melt in a warm south wind. One fine day he observed that the guard no longer squatted in the snow outside his lodge. Blinking in unaccustomed sunlight, he stood at the doorflap, shading his eyes with a hand. In sudden resolve, blanket thrown about his shoulders, he stepped into a kind of Indian summer, as it was called back in Springfield. Now there was irony in the term.

The camp was a beehive of activity. People wandered about, laughing, talking with friends, renewing acquaintances. In high spirits the blotched wiry ponies frisked in the brush corral. An old man sat in the sun, working with a pile of brass tubes; the Oglalas saved and reloaded their shells. A herald in a blue Union forage cap rode about the camp, apparently calling out the news.

Enjoying the stretching of his long legs, Sam wandered uncertainly through the soggy meadow, boots squishing in the mud. "Ma'am," he said politely to a matron hacking at a frozen deer haunch. "Nice day!" But the woman only stared at him, hand clapped over her mouth, and then rushed inside the lodge. Her dog bared teeth at him and snarled.

When he turned, he saw a crowd of urchins following him; they scattered and ran, a covey of birds suddenly disturbed.

"Come back!" he called, beckoning. He liked children and did not want even Indian children to run from him. After all, *they* did not yet scalp and murder. But the children were fearful, resuming the distant trailing only when he plodded on.

Avoiding the great lodge where he had confronted Buffalo Horns that night, he sat on a ledge of rock to remove his boots and wring out sodden socks. The children edged nearer, watching him. When he beckoned they scattered again, returning to eye him from the cover of stunted junipers and stands of winter-killed willows along the frozen stream.

"Suit yourself," he grumbled, grateful for the warm sun on his back. At least, he was no longer an actual prisoner.

Sitting for a long time, eyes half-closed, he drowsed in the warmth, thinking of Cletus Wiley. Was there a chance the old man might pass by this Indian camp, trade for him or somehow gain his freedom? Possible, Sam supposed. But—freedom for what? To go home again, humiliated by the failure of his practice, hounded by unpaid debts?

Aware the winter sun was sliding down the western escarpments of the Chetish, he stood up, pulling the blanket around his shoulders. The people had gone back into warm lodges; a pall of haze from cooking fires drifted low among the trees. The sun was a red ball in a smoky western sky. Stalking along the path, lost in thought, he turned suddenly at the feeling he was being followed.

Old Buffalo Horns stood behind him, painted face malevolent. As Sam stared, the old man shook the buffalo-tail switch in Sam's face and did a small shuffling dance. Quickly he reached into a hide pouch under his arm and flung a pinch of yellowish dust.

"Stop that!" Sam protested and sneezed hard.

Buffalo Horns chanted in a high-pitched voice—a string of curses, Sam supposed. When he took a threatening step forward, Buffalo Horns danced nimbly aside, continuing to deliver his imprecations.

"Old faker!" Sam muttered and turned his back. When he reached his own lodge the shaman had disappeared. *Gone*, Sam thought savagely. *Gone to plot against me!* With his electrical medicine he had certainly made an enemy of old Buffalo Horns.

Sweet Grass Woman awaited him, stirring a pot of stew with a long wooden spoon. The child—Chickadee—played at her feet, hitching himself about on his crippled foot as he stacked old bones to make a miniature tipi. *Hungry?* she asked Sam, making the sign —flat of hand in a sawing motion across her stomach.

Sam squatted, nodding. He had managed to pick up some of the *wibluta*, the hand language. The gestures were quick and effective. By now he and Sweet Grass Woman could carry on a rudimentary conversation, though the Sioux tongue itself sounded like gibberish, with no Greek or Latin roots to help. But with her aid, and occasional assistance from Growler and her brother, young Dancer, he mastered a few of the spoken words. Corn, dried corn, was something like *waka maza*. *Bello* were dried potatoes. *Tollo* was meat; that was easy to say. It was the staple of diet—buffalo meat, dried, or dug up frozen from pits in the earth where they cached it. Coffee, scarce in the camp, was *pazuta sapa*. And *wakan*—that was a kind of portmanteau word. It seemed to signify anything puzzling, mysterious, perhaps spiritual or otherworldly. The Oglalas prayed to Wakan Tanka, a great spirit. Horses were *shonka wakan* —as near as Sam could figure out, that meant The Great Spirit's

Dogs. Always of an inquiring bent, Sam was intrigued by the picturesque figure of speech.

"Hie," he said when she brought him supper. *Thanks.*

After supper, Sweet Grass Woman lit a kerosene lamp and brought out a well-thumbed deck of playing cards. She loved to play cards, trying to teach him a game something like rummy, though he had never understood the rules. But he pushed the cards away, wanting to talk. *The people,* he gestured. Improvising, signing a stew of Oglala signs and deaf-mute talk, he managed to make himself understood. *The people. Left Hand. Do they like me?*

Biting her lip, she frowned, following his awkward gestures. At last her eyes lit in comprehension. She shifted the sleeping Chickadee to her other arm.

Afraid!

What will they do with me? he asked.

For a long time she puzzled over this, not comprehending, or unwilling to say.

She laid the sleeping child down, covering it with a small blanket of rabbitskins sewn together. Avoiding his eyes, she arranged the folds of the blanket, patting it here, pulling at it there.

What will they do with me? Angry, frustrated, he grasped her arm.

Slowly she turned stricken eyes toward him. Did she understand his words? Was there something she did not want to tell him? When she remained silent, he thrust her away and squatted moodily beside the dying fire.

Sweet Grass Woman slept on a robe at the far circumference of the lodge, modestly distant from his own slatted bed. Although at first he was uneasy at the idea of a female, even a Sioux squaw, close by, he now had adapted to her presence. Sweet Grass Woman was a widow, he learned from Growler; the situation was not quite so embarrassing as it might have been. Lying sleepless and worried in the night, he knew from her restrained breathing she was also awake.

What was he to do? He suspected from their conversation there was something unpleasant in store for him; they were trying to make up their minds. Buffalo Horns certainly hated him. The people feared him. The short respite with Sweet Grass Woman was probably only a prelude to some gory end. Remembering Cletus Wiley's stories of Sioux tortures, he worried. Growler was his only hope.

Nervous, he jumped when Sweet Grass Woman crawled to him. Weeping, she pressed a tear-stained face against his.

Startled, he said, "Here, now!"

With gentle fingers she stroked his stubbled cheek.

"Love," she murmured in English.

He had not known she knew any English words other than "eat."

"Love?" he asked, uncomfortable.

With a rising inflection, obviously a question, she repeated the word. Stubborn, he drew back from her. "What do you mean?"

In the red glow of the dying fire her eyes were moist, luminous. He felt her body sleek against his. Her scent—sweet grasses?—invaded his nostrils, his brain, his will; not a Paris scent, certainly, but powerfully stimulating.

"No!" he protested.

This was an Indian woman, a *squaw!* He became giddy, as if he lost his way and stumbled unknowing to the edge of an abyss.

"No," he repeated, this time with less conviction.

Still she clung tightly to him. Struggling against his animal nature, he made a halfhearted attempt to pull away. But it was no good. Finally he put his arms about her and buried his lonely face in the sweet-smelling hair. He forgot Sweet Grass Woman was a squaw, forgot about all the host of deadly venereal diseases. She was a woman.

After interminable weeks awaiting the pleasure of Left Hand and his counselors, something happened to remind Sam he remained in danger. Sentence deferred or not, electrical magic or no, Growler his friend or enemy, fate could strike him down at any time. These Oglalas were bloodthirsty savages. His life meant no more to them than the life of the Crow who stumbled accidentally on the village.

Lost and hungry, the young brave was captured and brought before Left Hand. Acting on the chief's negligent gesture, the Oglala women and children bound the Crow to a post, passing their time by pricking him with knives and poking burning brands into his skin.

Bravely the Crow bore the torture, shouting taunts and obsceni-
ties at his tormentors. They jeered back, part of the deadly game.
Finally, tiring of the fun, someone cut off the Crow's head. A
gleeful squaw kicked it into a snowbank. The headless body was
propped against a tree; children, with tiny play bows, shot sharpened sticks into it until the trunk looked like a porcupine.

Sam, revolted at the sight, sat nervously in the tipi, watching
Sweet Grass Woman feed Chickadee a bowl of gruel. From his
face, she seemed to know what was troubling him. Finishing the
feeding, she left Chickadee to play with a wooden top and sat beside him.

"*Absaroka*," she murmured.

He understood that was what the Sioux called the Crow people.

"Absaroka," she repeated, gesturing toward the meadow where
the young man had died. She made a sign for *bad:* clenched hands
held before her breast, then the hands suddenly snapped outward,
fingers extended. *Bad. Bad Crow! Crows are bad!*

How lightly she took all this! Crows are bad. The Crows are to
be killed. Nothing personal—only part of a familiar ritual. Sam
shuddered, knowing he could be killed as brutally, as casually.
White men. Bad. White is bad. The logic could be the same.

So nearly as Sam could figure out, Sweet Grass Woman was
Growler's niece. "She baby my brother," Growler had said. He
visited Sam's lodge often, being fond of little Chickadee. But as
Sam later discovered, his interest in the child was more than
familial. Sweet Grass Woman brewed tea for Sam and her uncle,
and often they jointly smoked a pipe filled with shaved willow
bark, white man's tobacco having become scarce. Sam did not care
for the stuff, but it was sensible to keep on Growler's good side. Except for the whiskers, Growler reminded him of Uncle Milo
Penrose, who often visited the Blair home of a Sunday to sit in the
parlor, drink tea, and smoke his pipe. Sam's mother was Uncle
Milo's sister.

"Snow come," Growler said conversationally, gesturing.

It was true; the brief Indian summer was coming to an end. Soon
the snows, real winter snows, would blanket the camp. Sam had
laid plans, plans that must be carried out soon—possibly this night
—if he were to take advantage of the unseasonable weather.

Covertly he had laid aside a small stock of food, hidden under a robe at the edge of the lodge. He had stored away also a sharp knife, a coil of rope braided from horsehair, and a block of sulphur matches.

"Foot," Growler said conversationally.

"Foot?" Sam asked. He had taught Growler a few English words, but he did not recall that *foot* was one of them.

"Foot," Sweet Grass Woman repeated. Chickadee in her arms, she held out the twisted member. "You—you—" Frustrated, she turned toward Growler for help.

Growler pointed to the Tractors. "Medicine," he said. "Big medicine!" He made a face, crossed his eyes, and swayed back and forth in imitation of old Buffalo Horns caught in the electric embrace of the Tractors. "Big medicine!" he repeated. "Wakan!" He took the child's foot in knotted brown fingers. "Fix?" he asked.

They thought he could cure that twisted foot with his Tractors! The simple faith touched him. Not finding the words or the signs, he fumbled for an explanation. "No, no!" he protested in English. "It doesn't work that way! They're for other things, you see—colic, female complaints, the scrofula—"

They didn't understand. Eagerly they watched, awaiting a favorable reaction from him.

"They're not for *that!*" He tried to sign his meaning, convince them the Tractors could not possibly cure Chickadee. But they only continued to stare.

"Oh, Christ!" Sam took refuge in profanity, a habit not customary with him. Wearily he shrugged. "All right!" He took Chickadee in his arms, fingers probing gently at the small twisted foot. The child lay contented in his arms, gurgling happily and drooling on Sam's jacket.

Phalanges, he thought, remembering old Professor Hinkle at the Academy, a stern taskmaster; *metatarsals, tarsus, talus, lateral malleolus, medial malleolus*—there was a scurrilous doggerel to aid medical students in remembering the order of the bones of the foot.

Growler was trying to explain to him Bird Talker had applied his own brand of Oglala medicine to the child's foot—dancing, sacred pollen, pounding the drum and singing—without result. Bird Talker was the shaman. Sam had known him for so long as Buffalo

Horns that he had trouble remembering the medicine man's actual name. Sam caught only snatches of Growler's explanation; he was too busy feeling the odd formation of the bone between the medial malleolus and the talus.

"Hmmmm," he mused.

Sweet Grass Woman and Growler looked at him as people have looked at doctors from time immemorial when the physician said "hmmmmm."

"I remember this thing," Sam muttered.

He closed his eyes, seeing in his mind the way the bones fit together, putting together a spatial picture of the junction of the malleolus and the talus. Professor Hinkle had demonstrated a case like this. Sam remembered the operating theater, a little girl on the table, old Hinkle with a scalpel on one hand and a pointer in the other, describing the malformation on a colored chart from Heaton's *Compendium of Surgical Practices*. *Bauer's Anomaly?* Some obscure misunion of the bones. Was that it?

Sweet Grass Woman touched his arm. It was a light touch but pleading more eloquent than if she had spoken.

"Well," Sam conceded, "it's a classic case, and the surgery is established." Aware he had lapsed into English, he tried a few Sioux words, along with gestures somewhat restricted because little Chickadee was hanging lovingly around his neck.

"Can fix?" Growler demanded, impatient.

As best he could, he explained that if Chickadee were in a white man's hospital with a proper operating theater, chloroform, a nurse, all the appurtenances, there was a fair chance a surgeon could stretch the tendons, fit the bones together properly. Then, with the foot in a plaster cast for a long time, the grotesque misalignment might be corrected, foot restored to something approaching normal function and weight-bearing. It was difficult; he was sweating and nervous before he finally made them understand.

"No fix!" Growler muttered.

Sweet Grass Woman knew the meaning of the sound of Growler's voice, if not the words. She began to weep, very softly. Chickadee, curious, turned bright eyes on her. Compassionate, he struggled to reach his mother. Sam let the child go. Chickadee hobbled to Sweet Grass Woman's lap, nestling his head against her breast.

"It needs a hell of a lot more than just a surgeon!" Sam insisted. "You've got to have proper facilities! You can't ask a man to operate in a damned tipi, can you? I'm sorry!" He made the sign—*heart laid on the ground*—a small circle with thumb and forefinger over the heart, then the hand swept outward, palm turned over. Sweet Grass Woman used it when she thought she had somehow offended him. Deaf-mutes, Sam remembered from Springfield days, held the palm of the right hand near the face, fingers extended. Then they lowered the hand, fingers curled, and inclined the head in sadness. He had come to prefer the Sioux version.

"*Why* no fix?" Growler demanded. He threw down his pipe, and the dottle began to burn a hole in a robe. Sweet Grass Woman hurried to extinguish it. "You medicine, big medicine!" He became angry, and pointed to the Tractors, to Sam's medical kit. "Big medicine! Wakan! *Why* no fix?"

Apparently Growler thought that because Sam's big medicine had vanquished Bird Talker, a powerful man in the tribe, it was sufficient to do more. Growler was a politician. Like the Roman senators of old, Sam read about in school, Growler knew the value of more bread and bigger circuses. Growler was certainly old Bird Talker's chief political rival among Left Hand's Oglalas.

"Look here," Sam said, trying to be reasonable. In a mix of English, Sioux, and *wibluta*, the hand language, he tried to explain. But Growler would have none of it. In spite of Sweet Grass Woman's gentle remonstrations, he finally knocked over his cup of tea and stalked from the lodge.

"Well," Sam muttered, "that's that!" Now he had made an enemy of Growler. His time was growing short.

Dusk came on. Sweet Grass Woman sat, head bowed, with the child in her arms. Uncomfortable, Sam left the tipi and walked to the edge of the surrounding woods to be alone with his thoughts. The western sky was streaked with horizontal lines of orange, red, and gunmetal gray. High over his head a V of geese rustled, honking as they winged south. Arms folded, he stood for a long time staring at the retreating ducks but hardly seeing them. There was chloroform in his medical kit and a full set of surgical instruments. On the other hand, why should he help an Indian child to walk? If he were successful, Chickadee would grow up to murder and scalp white settlers like Clara Freeman's father. At twelve or thirteen he would, according to Cletus Wiley, go into the mountains naked and hungry to dream a vision, coming back as Red Knife or Walking Horse or some other appropriate name. Then he would be a man, a warrior, a letter of white man's blood.

Taking a deep breath, Sam looked down at his hands. They were big bony hands, but clever; he trusted them. He was a good surgeon. He could do it. But what if the operation failed? Suppose Chickadee sickened, took a fever, died? Things would go hard with Sam Blair then, like the unfortunate Crow captured near the camp. Besides—he stiffened at the thought that came to him. Sweet Grass Woman; she loved him, she had said. But maybe that had been just a trick, a sleazy Indian trick, to enlist his sympathy for Chickadee! He did not want to believe it, but it could be true. Indians were not white people. They did not have a well-developed sense of morality.

Apprehensive, perplexed, he became aware the wind was rising. Looking into the star-sprinkled night, he realized he had been standing there for a long time. He was shivering, his feet were cold. He was miserable; not only his body, but his mind. What was he to do?

Searching for Orion's belt, low on the horizon at this hour, he could not find it. Then he realized it was obscured by a bank of clouds on the eastern horizon. Finally he came to a conclusion. All this thinking about Chickadee and Sweet Grass Woman was pointless. He had no time for surgery. While the good weather held, he must flee the camp.

Listening, he heard a faint rhythmic throbbing. Someone was pounding a drum in Left Hand's big lodge in the center of the meadow. A big shivaree seemed to be going on. Even now they might be making their decision. Perhaps old Bird Talker was haranguing, speechifying, arguing the white man was bad luck and ought now to be burned to death. Sam Blair's medicine had run out.

That night, while Chickadee and Sweet Grass Woman slept, he bundled the carefully hoarded provisions in a deerhide and slipped from the tipi. His medical kit, the unpaid-for Tractors—all these he had to leave behind. It agonized him, but he had to travel light if he were to escape a horrible fate.

At the corral he thought briefly of trying to steal a horse. He had always been knowledgeable about horseflesh, but Indian ponies were fractious; he abandoned the idea and trudged into the surrounding trees. It started to snow, the lightest, most delicate of downpours. That was not necessarily bad. It would soon hide any tracks he left.

CHAPTER 4

He had miscalculated, and the price of the miscalculation was his life. When he departed the Oglala village, unnoticed and unmissed, the snow was only a faint white downpour through which he could see a full moon, surrounded by a luminous halo. The air was cold and crisp. Tiny flakes touched his lips and brow, with no hint of danger. But now that he emerged from the trees and shivered in the cold blast combing the rocky ledges of the Chetish, he knew he had been a fool.

From the canyons below the wind howled up at him, a fierce beast seeking only to destroy. The gale tore at his clothes, almost pulled the blanket from his shoulders. Icy particles of sleet stung his cheeks and exposed hands. The beneficent moon waned. Alone, terribly alone, he braced himself against the storm.

Down there, that way—was that not how the Oglalas had first come, from below? There was a cleft in the rocks and a jumble of boulders he thought he remembered, evidence of a recent slide. Looking in the other direction, however, he saw in the waning moonlight a blasted tree, hit by lightning, and remembered that too.

Which way to go? Or either way? Perhaps it was best to hole up in the washed-away roots of a giant spruce rearing like a sentinel at the edge of the ridge.

Cowed by the angry winds, he sank down among the tangle of roots, deerhide bag in his lap, and pulled the precious blanket tightly about him. For several minutes he squatted, listening to the skreeling of the wind. Suddenly he tensed, feeling the frigid flesh crawl. Something was in the makeshift shelter with him. He heard a noise, a coughing growl, and the hairs prickled on the back of his neck.

Paralyzed with fear, he sat immobile. A bear? Sometimes they made winter dens in hollow trees, Cletus said. Or maybe a cougar, what was called in the Territory a painter. Or—

When the animal grunted again, closer, he sprang from the cage of roots like a flying squirrel, arms and legs spread. Landing in a snowdrift, he gasped for breath as nose and mouth filled with snow. Shaking his head wildly, he came to hands and knees, hoping the animal was not pursuing. But the upturned tree showed only a dark tangle of roots, a black hole in the surrounding drifts. Cautiously he got to his feet, grateful he had saved the blanket. The deerhide bag, however, was still in the mass of twisted roots. He did not intend to go back for it.

Heart pounding from the escape, he staggered down the slope toward the lightning-blasted tree. Yes, that was the tree; he was certain of it!

Now the winds moderated, but snow fell more heavily. He floundered in a snowy morass. At times he was not sure whether he burrowed through the snow or labored atop it. Below, in the blackness, lay the valley of the Yellowstone. Down there were houses, a glow of lamplight on snow, brassy pots of hot water ready to brew tea. Although snow fell more heavily, at least he was going downhill. All he had to do was stagger forward, one foot before the other, until he reached warmth and safety. Hot tea, with biscuits, of course; he thought of Ma Bidwell's biscuits, brown and crisp on top, soft and smoking within. Biscuits, biscuits with honey—an amber oozing penetrating each crack and fissure of the virgin surface.

Inattentive, he fell again, sprawling flat into a cottony sea. This time he lay for a long time, struggling weakly. How foolish he had been, to daydream about tea and biscuits and honey! This was *real*, this was life and death in a Territorial winter! He had better get on his feet and think only of survival!

Still, it was not too bad in the snowbank. He lay quietly, feeling somehow warm. His cheeks burned; maybe that was frostbite. But they *did* feel warm. Perhaps it was a good idea to rest for a while.

Lying in the snow he thought longingly of the past; a summer evening on the Freeman's veranda, Clara and he sitting on the steps. Mrs. Freeman made a pitcher of sassafras tea cooled by ice brought from the sawdust-lined pit dug in a hillside. Each winter Mr. Freeman had cut ice from the river.

"Clara," Sam murmured. He held his glass to her lips, and she held hers to his own. It was a daring thing to do, with her father smoking his pipe nearby. "Clara," he said, "I love you."

She rose then, walking down the long veranda, and beckoned him to follow. He tried to rise, but his limbs were like boiled noodles, and he fell back. "Clara," he murmured. "Oh, Clara!" He wept.

Then a stern voice broke in on his hopelessness. Oddly enough, it was his own. Sam Blair was talking to Sam, or however it should be said.

"Get up," the voice said. "Stop this damned dreaming! Man, you're freezing to death!"

"I'm tired," Sam protested.

"You'll have one hell of a long sleep if you don't get up!" the voice insisted. "Is this what you saved and worked and went to school for—to lie down in a snowbank and dream yourself to death?"

"Clara," he murmured feebly.

The voice snarled. "Clara Freeman isn't here! She's going to marry Andy Wyatt and go to Washington to live!" The voice turned softer, more persuasive. "What about your pa and ma? They worked their fingers to the bone to help you through the Academy, become a doctor. Is that all it meant to you? Get up!"

There was something to what the voice said. Still and all, it was comfortable in the fleecy bank.

"Remember Professor Tollefson's book?" the voice wheedled. "*The Manual of Arctic Surgery?* It tells how Russian peasants lie down and go to sleep and they find them later, frozen so hard they stack the bodies like cordwood till the ground thaws in the spring."

Remembering the gruesome drawings in Professor Tollefson's book, he shuddered. It was true, he realized; he was lying dreamily in the snow, hypnotized, waiting for death.

"That's right," he agreed. "Sam, you're perfectly right! I'm glad you brought that up!"

With a great effort he struggled to his feet. Somewhere he had lost his blanket. Swaying, he looked down at the black image pressed into the snow where he had recently lain. Hobson's choice:

lie down again or be recaptured by the Oglalas? Still and all, what
would they want of him? Why would they come after him, a white
man who had only been a burden and probably an embarrassment?

Stop thinking, he told himself. *Thinking won't get you out of this.
Just keep going—one foot in front of the other.* But somewhere he
had lost his boot again. *No matter. Keep on walking.*

Incredibly, he was still staggering forward when the eastern escarpment of the Chetish flushed with dawn. Propped against a tree,
murmuring nonsense rhymes, he peered at the pockmarked face
confronting him.

"Growler," he remarked.

A pony was tied nearby. Growler, in bearskin robe and fur hat,
caught him as he slipped down against the trunk of the tree.

"Back," the Oglala grunted. "We go—back. Home!"

Sam Blair, tied in place on the pony with a braided hair rope,
blinked down at his rescuer. Ice so caked his beard and mouth it
was hard to talk.

"Home?" he mumbled. "Home?"

Growler didn't answer. Instead, he took the pony's hackamore
and trudged back the snowy trail toward the Oglala village.

Fortunately, he did not damage himself too much in the aborted
escape. He caught cold and was tormented by the aftereffects of
frostbite: itching, peeling skin, and a bone-deep throbbing. But an
old woman named Big Throat plastered his hands and feet with
poultices of dried sage leaves crushed in a stone mortar and damp-
ened with tea, a commodity precious among the Oglalas. It
relieved the itching greatly, though he had no idea of how it
worked. At the Blair home, sage was usually something to flavor the
stuffing in the Thanksgiving turkey when his folks could afford one.
Still, he was whole and viable, though still a captive in a hostile Indian camp. The snows were now so deep that no one in his right
mind could think about escaping until spring, at least; spring, that
was to say, unless by then Sam Blair had been destroyed on some
savage whim.

Wrapped in his blanket, he watched Sweet Grass Woman carving
chops from a frozen deer haunch for his supper. The Oglalas
wrapped fresh meat in buffalo hides and buried it in the ground to

preserve it for winter use, when game was scarce. To keep away wandering wolves attracted by the blood, they soaked wet rags in gunpowder and tied them to sticks driven into the ground around the site. Sam, feet still painful, hobbled toward Sweet Grass Woman.

"Let me do that!" he insisted, reaching for the hatchet.

She was obdurate. By signs she made him know he was still sick; anyway, this was woman's work. Her skin was suffused by a rosy glow, and congealed breath surrounded her head in a misty halo. Actually, she seemed to be enjoying herself. Did she love him so much she had sent Growler to fetch him from the snow? That was unlikely. He had to admit he was no great catch, even to an Indian squaw; all they wanted was for him to cure little Chickadee.

In the tipi he spooned up the rich meat stew, laced with beans of some kind and potatolike roots he could not identify. "Hie," he said, bobbing his head. "Hie, hie."

Maybe Growler had brought him back for his own purposes. Growler, both in manner and appearance, reminded Sam of a fellow student in medical school. Abner Dirks had as little money as Sam. Abner, however, was a lot smarter. He organized raffles, was amateur veterinarian to ailing cows, won small stakes at whist and cooncan, and traded everything from Barlow knives to brood mares. Abner often lent less prosperous classmates money, and when Sam left for the West, was running for the Illinois Legislature. Growler, likewise, seemed to be a kind of politician about the camp. Maybe Growler was saving Sam for possible political capital. Sam's long and unkempt hair crawled with the possibilities.

"Like?" Bemused, he stared at her for a moment. When she indicated the empty wooden bowl, he remembered his manners.

"I like," he said. "Sure enough." Then he remembered the Sioux words. "*Sha, sha,*" he nodded. "*Sha, sha, sha!*" The word *sha* seemed to mean *red*, a color dear to the Oglalas; *sha sha*, the words repeated, meant *excellent*.

She made a sign, then—one he did not understand—wrists crossed over full breasts and pressed to her heart. The gesture probably had something to do with affection, because that night, when she lay with him, Sweet Grass Woman was very loving.

Her brother, the slender young man named Dancer, one day

brought Sam a tattered book, demanding to be shown how to read.
The book was a dogeared copy of Sir Walter Scott's *Ivanhoe*. An in-
scription on the flyleaf said "To Cora Witherspoon from Papa and
Mama on her Twelfth Birthday, April 16th, 1861." Probably, Sam
thought, the volume was seized from a ravished settler's cabin.
Where now was Cora Witherspoon? He hoped her bones were not
whitening in a forest glade along the river.

"You've got to learn your ABCs first," Sam explained.

Dancer, a mild and pleasant youth who would not have looked
out of place in steel-rimmed spectacles, did not understand. But
Sam soon had him scrawling the letters of the alphabet in the blank
pages at the end of the book, delighted when Sam gave him good
grades. Dancer also brought Sam an old calendar, perhaps taken
also from the Witherspoon cabin. Sam cut it up to make a crude
notebook in which he scribbled his impressions of captivity.
Though he knew it was a lost cause, he wrote his comments in the
form of a letter to Clara Freeman:

Dear Clara:

Well, here I am in the Strangest Circumstances ever a man
was. I am caught by the Oglala Indians and confined to their
camp in the Chetish Mountain by a Dreadful Set of events I
will not now go into but will explain if ever I see you again,
which is not likely, I fear.

They treat me well enough so far but I fear I am like a prize
steer being fattened for some Savage Barbecue.

A woman cooks for me and mends my clothes, which are
now ragged. I piece them out with odds and ends given to me
so I am now beginning to look like a Sioux Myself! I walk
about the camp but someone is always watching me. I tried to
escape once but they brought me back pretty quick.

In spite of my Perilous Condition I watch what goes on and
try to learn. It is a strange society, in some ways not so
different from Fitch's Landing, or Springfield, for that matter.
The women sew and chat, the children play games, the men
dress in fine clothes like Society Dudes, and play Politics. They
like Tea and Tobacco and Raisins as we do, which they get
from the white men when they are on good terms with them. I
mean there is a lot of trouble between the Indians and the

white man, whom the Oglalas call The People With Hats. There is bound to be a Big Fight in the spring. I see sort of Ambassadors come from other tribes and they all get together in the Chief's big lodge and argue and wrangle all day long. I think they are Laying Plans for a big fracas when the snow disappears.

He read over what he had written. *A woman cooks for me and mends my clothes.* Sweet Grass Woman did a great deal more than that for him. Still, he did not consider it politic to go into that, though no white face was likely ever to gaze on the pages.

> She is a widow—the woman I mean—and reminds me in some ways of you. She has a little boy, Chickadee; he has a twisted foot. I fear for him because when he grows up he will be no good to them as a Warrior. They have few Finer Sensibilities, and I can imagine them some day driving him away because he is a Burden. It is very Sad.

Each day he wrote in the journal and soon began to run out of paper. Dancer scoured the camp and brought back a miscellaneous collection of scraps which Sam pieced out with scraped remnants of deerhide, even paper-thin rolls of bark peeled from the birches surrounding the camp. The journal grew and became an odd-looking but voluminous book.

One day he was writing feverishly when Growler and Dancer appeared. Ceremonially, dressed in best finery, they squatted as on a Sunday call. Growler wore a shirt of mountain-sheep skin with trailing fringes, colored quillwork across shoulders and chest, with tassels of hair—scalps?—on either side. Fine leggings of buckskin adorned his wiry legs, a broad-beaded stripe down each side and a heavy twisted fringe from knee to ankle. Dancer sported a scarlet trailing breech clout a foot wide, reaching to the ground. A necklace of bear claws hung on the hairless chest, and he wore moccasins covered with elaborate designs in colored beads. Sweet Grass Woman, Sam suddenly noticed, had a new deerskin dress. Her long braids were wrapped in otter fur and tied with a red ribbon.

"What is all this?" Sam asked.

The child, Chickadee, too, was dressed to the nines in a long

buckskin shirt, softened to almost clothlike texture by Sweet Grass
Woman's patient chewing; a sash of precious red cloth belted the
garment at his waist. Chickadee, however, was not feeling well.
The deformed foot obviously bothered him, the flesh red and
inflamed in spite of old Big Throat's poultices.

"What is all this?" Sam repeated, feeling a chill wash his stomach. He turned to Sweet Grass Woman. She was cooking several
pots bubbling on the fire at once. A ceremonial feast was being
prepared. In prisons the condemned man was given a last meal of
his choice. Was this—the end?

"You," Growler muttered. "You." He pointed to Sam.

"Me?"

"We think about you," Growler said. "We—we think. What you
say."

Sam accepted the bowl of corn and beans handed him. There
were the usual roots, also, but sliced thin and cooked in a precious
can of Blue Hen tomatoes. Slabs of buffalo hump, edged with crisp
brown fat, were pressed on him. Somewhere, Sweet Grass Woman
had found coffee, real coffee, and there was a whole potful.

"I don't know what this is all about," Sam protested, wiping his
greasy mouth with the back of a tattered sleeve.

Growler belched, patted his stomach, lit a pipe. Dancer sighed,
satiated, smoked also. Sweet Grass Woman tried to feed Sam a tid-
bit from her own bowl, but he was stuffed.

"Medicine," Growler remarked. Reverentially he held up the
Magnetic Tractors. "Big medicine!" He opened Sam's black satchel
and laid out the pills, the ointments, the powders; the bone saw,
scalpel, retractors. "More medicine! Big medicine!"

"We've been through all that!" Sam protested.

"Wait!" Growler held up a hand. "Bird Talker—" He made the
sign for *bird*, then opened hinged hands in *talk*; he was referring to
the Oglala medicine man who so disliked Sam. "Bird Talker medicine no good." Growler pointed to Chickadee's twisted foot, and the
child whimpered. "No—no fix. He no can fix. No good!"

Sam understood. At one time or another, the old shaman had
tried his medicine on the child's foot without success.

"No good," he agreed.

"You fix!" Growler insisted. "You! Big medicine!"

"It's impossible!" Sam protested. "Big medicine or no, I'm not God! Don't you understand?"

This time Growler would not be denied. Like a dog with a bone, he continued the argument. At first Sam did not realize what Growler was saying, in guttural English and Sioux and rapid signs. Then he began to catch the gist of the argument.

Bird Talker hates you! Bird Talker says you do not have medicine, real medicine! He says if you cannot fix the boy's foot you should be killed, your head cut off, your body left for the children to shoot arrows at, like that Crow man! I tell you again! Fix the boy's foot, or—

Sam swallowed hard. He was frightened. Better he might have died in the snow! The snow was not so bad—really, warm and rather comfortable.

"All right," he muttered. He had learned the sign for *agreed* and made it—fingers touching his temples, then both hands spread down and outward before his chest. *Our minds are the same; agreed.* Death had brushed him by in the snow. Now death was stalking him again. But danger or not, he had taken an oath to relieve suffering; he was still a physician.

On a sunny winter day he laid out his instruments on a pilfered white man's table. It was too dark in the lodges, so Chickadee lay outdoors on a kind of litter fashioned for the occasion. The litter was propped up on empty ammunition boxes, probably stolen from a supply train inching along from Fort Buford on the Missouri. Chickadee was frightened. His baby eyes rolled, and he tried to escape from the table. Sweet Grass Woman spoke softly and restrained him. Growler, the boy's great-uncle, stood nearby, dangling a cornhusk doll to divert him.

"Keep him still," Sam ordered, opening his bottle of chloroform to moisten a clean rag. "Tell him I'm not going to hurt him. Tell him to smell this rag, how funny it smells—kind of sweet, like a pretty flower."

The Oglalas had assembled to watch the operation. Left Hand himself sat on a throne of boxes draped with a scarlet blanket. Old Bird Talker, grinning contemptuously, sat next to him, murmuring to the chief behind his hand. The members of the various secret societies—the Silent Talkers, the Bad Faces, the Fox Soldiers—kept order in the crowd. The rocky bowl serving as an operating theater was small. People crowded close to the table, perched on boulders, climbed trees for a better view. Sam Blair's medicine was again to be tested.

At first Chickadee struggled briefly. With Growler holding him and Sweet Grass Woman talking to the child in her soft voice, his struggles gradually weakened. Sam, nervous, let fall another few drops of the clear liquid on the cloth masking the small face.

Finally the child lay still. Sam pulled aside the cloth, opened an eyelid, stared at the dilated pupils. Chickadee slept. Sweet Grass Woman, seeing the child unmoving and lifeless, began to worry. But Sam smiled and put a hand on hers. "Sleep," he explained. "He sleeps." He made the simple sign, familiar to him when his deaf-mute parents wanted him to go to bed—right hand, palm to cheek, and head bent slowly to the right. "He will wake soon."

He had borrowed a sewing needle and thread from old Big Throat, the old woman with the goiter who prepared the sage poultices for his frostbitten hands and feet. Now, squinting in the winter sun, he picked up his Sölingen scalpel and measured with his eye the incision he would make in the baby foot. *Metatarsals, tarsus, talus, lateral malleolus, medial malleolus*—he closed his eyes, imagining the sequence of bones, ligaments, blood vessels. In ragged shirt sleeves, he was none the less sweating.

In sudden resolve he lowered the scalpel and began—a long slice down the instep. Blood bubbled out. There was an immediate intake of breath from the spectators. "Hand me that rag!" he ordered Sweet Grass Woman, and swabbed blood from the wound.

He cut deeper, spreading the wound with retractors, summoning Growler to hold them in place. Growler looked pale. In spite of his fears, Sam almost grinned. Growler might be a great warrior, but this was Sam Blair's battleground.

Sweet Grass Woman's face was tense with anxiety, but she hovered obediently near Sam, handing him rags and instruments as he indicated. Once, hurrying, he cut too deep and blood spouted. Quickly he tied off the severed vessel with Big Throat's thread, but the sight of so much blood unnerved the spectators. Left Hand frowned, Bird Talker urging him to interfere and save the child from the crazy white man. But as the gout bubbled and died, the chief sank back, gesturing for silence.

Bauer's Anomaly, Sam thought. Whoever Bauer had been, he had never seen an anomaly until he operated on a Sioux boy's foot in a hostile Indian camp, surrounded by spectators capable of torturing and killing the surgeon if the operation did not come off! But as he probed deeper, laying aside muscles and tendons to expose the basic architecture of the small foot, he became too interested in what he was doing to worry.

There! Foot laid bare, he poked thrice-washed fingers into the wound, clearing away the debris to examine the interlocking bones. Bauer's Anomaly! There it was, exactly as illustrated in Heaton's *Compendium of Surgical Practice;* instead of lying in a smooth progression, the bones were jumbled and misshapen, lying helterskelter as they progressed from the condyles of the tibia. It was as if a Roman arch had suddenly fallen and the stones, including the all-important keystone, lay in ruins.

Using one of his precious clean rags to wipe sweat from his brow, he wondered how anyone could fit those misaligned bones into a normal alignment? He wished Professor Bauer were beside him for a consultation. Sweet Grass Woman, seeing his dismay, spoke softly. He did not understand the words, but she was probably affirming trust in his skills.

"All right," he muttered. "All right, Sam! Don't stand here and mope! You call yourself a surgeon—get in there and go to work!"

Aware of restlessness in the crowd, he pried at the bones with his fingers, coaxing here, forcing there. They obstinately refused to do his bidding. Taking his scalpel and small saw, he cut away the malformations hindering the alignment of the tarsus and talus. Sweat dripped from his forehead into the wound. Perhaps attracted by the smell of blood, crows congregated in the trees and cawed. A cloud crossed the sun and shadows fell on his work; a bad omen? Still he labored at the tricky job, fitting, trimming, adjusting, like a tailor with a bolt of cloth for an important customer.

"Go *in* there!" he said between clenched teeth, forcing the misaligned bones. "God damn it, *go!*"

The crowd muttered, uneasy at the way Chickadee lay still and white-faced, while the white shaman cut and probed in the small foot. Chickadee was dead, obviously; how could anyone lie still with a foot horribly wounded, bones laid bare to the sun?

A good doctor was a mechanic at times; no less a mechanic than a wheelwright or a cabinetmaker. And now Sam was doing mechanic's work, as one fixes a broken wagon tongue. But if the wagon tongue could not be repaired, the farmer could buy a new one. No one would reproach the mechanic.

"No good," Growler muttered. Still holding the retractors, he turned a worried face on Sam. "No fix!" He nodded toward the small pale face. "Dead!"

Sam shook his head. "No, he's not dead! Just hang on to those retractors!" He gestured. "Pull that one—spread the cut so I can get my fingers in under the lateral malleolus!" When Growler hesitated, Sam shouted at him. "Do what I say, damn it!"

Finally he had it—thought he had it. But the whole complex structure popped apart, and he started again. Left Hand rose, folded his arms, looked down appraisingly. Old Bird Talker whispered and looked down sidewise at Sam, grinning like a gargoyle.

"Just a minute!" Sam begged. "Give me another minute or so! I've almost got it!"

This time he *did* have it. Triumphantly he got the errant bones in place, pushed the ligaments back, folded the severed tissues over the bones, picked up thread and the needle. He wished Professor Bauer had been there to see him close. As he pulled the last stitch tight, Chickadee stirred briefly, whimpered.

"There!" Sam shouted. He turned to the spectators. "He's not dead! I told you! Medicine—white man's medicine! *Big* medicine!"

Carefully he wrapped the small leg and foot, binding strips of precious trade gingham around makeshift splints fashioned from buffalo rib bones softened in boiling water and straightened. Chickadee whimpered again, opened puzzled eyes, put up a hand to shade his face from the strong light. Quickly Sweet Grass Woman put her cheek against his, making small cooing noises.

"That'll do it!" Sam gasped.

Trembling, sweating, he sat on a rocky ledge. Growler lifted the boy in his arms and carried him away to bed. Sweet Grass Woman, torn, stood beside Sam for a long time. Then, overcome, she rushed to be with her child. The crowd waited respectfully until Left

Hand rose, wrapped in his blanket, and stalked away, followed by his retinue. The people left too, drifting away in twos and threes, glancing covertly at Sam Blair and whispering.

Alone now, he sat for a long time in the sunlight. Finally he rose and gathered up the litter of instruments, bloody leftover splints and bindings. He had done what he could. Chickadee's fate, and his own, lay with the gods. Gangrene—a likely consequence of the surgery—would kill the child and Sam Blair also. But he hoped, both for himself and for the child.

CHAPTER 5

Left Hand's village lay buried in snow. Drifts covered the base of the tipis to a height of three or four feet. In the meadow, where the winter winds had full sway, the snow mounded in fantastic whorls and towers. In the brush corral the ponies subsisted on cottonwood twigs and branches, which were cut daily, some up to two inches in diameter but relished by the hungry animals. In the skin lodges the people remained snug and warm, with plenty of food, and games to play.

Sam was not sure of the date but figured it was nearing the Christmas season. To the Sioux it was *The Moon When Deer Shed Their Horns*. It had been over a week since he operated on Chickadee's crippled foot and the child was approaching a critical stage. The wound had not healed as Sam had hoped; it was edged with yellow pus, and beyond the incision lay parallel streaks of dark red, shading into black. Chickadee was feverish. Sweet Grass Woman held him in her arms to quiet his fretting. When she looked at Sam in supplication, he could only mutter reassurance; hope, hope against the gangrene he feared. *The operation was a success, but the patient died.* It had been a bad joke in medical school.

On a windy afternoon he squatted near the fire and wrote in his journal. Chickadee slept. Sweet Grass Woman, menstruating, had according to custom been banished to the outlying tipis called the Moon Lodges until she was again clean. In the interim old Big Throat cared for the child. Sam gnawed a point to the precious pencil and began:

Clara, it is Surprising how warm a tipi can be in the middle of Winter. The Sioux have a System that would do Benjamin Franklin proud. They bring in outside air through a rock-lined

Tunnel to the base of the fire. It is warmed there and rises to the Smoke-Vent above, where Careful Control restrains it from escaping Excessively. The interior becomes somewhat Smoky at times. I feel I am cured like a Virginia Ham. Really I remain quite Comfortable.

Chickadee woke. Big Throat cradled him, crooned. Sam resumed his writing:

An old woman—she has a Goiter which is repulsive in appearance but a sweet Soul—is my medical assistant. She knows a great deal about Herbs. When the baby I told you about began to suffer from inflammation of the wound she persuaded me to pack the leg with a poultice of wild garlic pounded into a paste and mixed with mud where we broke the Ice and dug into the riverbank. Also, she made a Potion from the leaves and stems of a Certain Plant—they call it *wan i o nots*—and gave it to the child. I can hardly Object, the boy is very sick and it is beyond my Power as a physician to help him further.

The old woman's crooning stilled Chickadee's complaints. She laid him tenderly down and bustled about fixing Sam's noonday meal; brown pemmican larded with buffalo tallow and spicy tart chokecherries, a big wooden bowl of crisp white *tipsin*, the Indian turnip, sliced thin and crunchy and dipped into the precious salt the Sioux obtained from an annual trip to the salt beds near the river. There was tea, also, but no sugar. Sugar, which the Oglalas loved, had run out. It was sorely missed.

After dinner Chickadee still slept. Relieved, Sam put on a heavy fur jacket and cap, wrapped a blanket about him, and floundered through the snow to breathe fresh air. For a while he helped Growler cut branches for the horses. But Growler, worried about Chickadee, was not communicative. Too, he was busy at his task; according to Sam's observations, there were as many as twenty horses per lodge, horses being a measure of a man's wealth. The great pony herd demanded a lot of forage.

Returning to the lodge in waning afternoon light, he had a curious feeling of being watched, followed. Frequently he wheeled, the hairs on the back of his neck prickling, but saw no one. The path around the great circle of lodges was deep-trodden with moccasins. Its beaten surface offered no clue.

Breath an icy vapor about his face, he examined the scene. No one; only tendrils of gray woodsmoke from the smoke vents, an occasional *thunk* as snow slid from an overloaded bough, a whinny from the corral as a playful pony bit another's rump. Growler had disappeared on some errand. The scene was tranquil, peaceful, like a print by Mr. Currier and Mr. Ives, whose artistry Sam admired. Uneasy, he trudged on.

Young Dancer waited in the lodge. Proudly he showed Sam the latest assignment—his own English name, printed in scrawling characters with a stub of charcoal on a board— D A N C E R .

"Good!" Sam smiled. "Very good! I'll give you an A on that!"

He was not prepared for the scream that followed. Old Big Throat pointed at him in horror. Dancer, too, paled, shrank back.

"What?" Sam asked. "What is it? What's wrong?"

His eye followed Big Throat's pointing finger. Twisting, he pulled at the hem of his fur jacket. In the heavy hairs of the pelt was caught a strange object. He jerked at it; a desiccated lizard. From it dangled a leather bag, attached by a bit of rawhide thong. The whole assembly clung to the fur like a burr. He had to work patiently until it came away in his hand.

"What in—" He stared at it while Big Throat wrung her hands and Dancer averted his eyes. "What is it?"

When he started to open the bag, Big Throat covered her face. Dancer made a ritual gesture of some sort to protect himself from evil.

"Magic?" Sam wondered. "Someone's medicine? A—a charm?"

He shook the contents of the bag into his palm: a few small pellets that looked like rabbit droppings, a bit of snakeskin, a mummified object that looked like—hastily he dropped it—a severed finger, shriveled and leathery.

"Bad!" Dancer quavered. "Oh, bad!"

Someone had sneaked up behind him and fastened the talisman to his coat, or perhaps hurled it from behind a snowbank. Bird Talker? It could have been. But with Chickadee ill, perhaps dying from the effects of Sam's surgery, it could have been anyone. In this savage society lineage was uncertain and poorly defined. Little

Chickadee had many uncles and aunts and cousins; they all loved the little boy. A curse on anyone who harmed him was probable.

"Look!" Sam protested. "This is silly! How can a bunch of junk hurt anyone? Why be afraid of it?"

Going to the doorflap, he hurled the stuff into the descending night. But when he came back into the tipi, dusting his hands with an air of finality, neither Big Throat nor Dancer would come near him. He had been somehow contaminated. Foolish as it all was, he was under no illusion as to the seriousness of his situation; his life hung by a thread.

Deprived of the companionship of Sweet Grass Woman, he was lonely. Sitting in his lodge, he stared at the fire. Chickadee was very low. The child's brow was fevered. Lips were drained of color, and the baby cheeks showed a yellowish waxen cast that unnerved Sam. He had seen too many people look like that, near the end. But there was nothing he could do. It was up to Chickadee to fight for his short life.

Old Big Throat sat by the child, from time to time turning a troubled look toward Sam. Hovering near the sickbed, she stirred powdered herbs into a tin cup of hot water. Still, Chickadee was Sam's patient! He rose and approached the old woman, by signs and stammered Sioux, demanding to know what was in the cup. But she drew away from him, uneasy, muttering gibberish he did not understand. Disconsolate, he withdrew and went back to squat by the fire. In Chickadee's perilous state, perhaps any medicine was better than to sit, as he was doing, and mope. To divert his thoughts from the dying child, he wrote again in his book:

The Sioux have a Great Regard for things that are Round. They pitch their Lodges in a circle, their Buffalo-skin Shields are round, the base of the Lodges is round, their Drums are Round, they keep to the Round wherever they can. Round is thought to be Good.

Gently Big Throat spooned green liquid into Chickadee's mouth. With great care and patience the old woman got most of the stuff into the child, all the time gently crooning. Sam shook his head and went on writing:

The Men are very Vain. On a nice Day they sit for hours before their Lodges primping, squatting on a blanket, combing their Hair, plucking out the Whiskers with clamshells used as Tweezers and painting their Faces. They like Fancy Clothes, and dress up all the Time. They have a lot of Clubs or Societies like the Freemasons or the Knights of Columbus or the Democrats. Even the boys have their Little Clubs, where they are taught early to be Strong and Brave and Disregard Pain and Suffering.

That night Sweet Grass Woman, risking both the menstrual taboo and the curse that lay on Sam, crept covertly into the lodge to visit her child. Big Throat, aghast at such temerity, scolded her. Sweet Grass Woman brushed her aside to hover over Chickadee.

"He is better!" she marveled.

Chickadee smiled weakly at her, put out a finger for her to hold.

"That's true," Sam said, puzzled.

"Sha," Big Throat beamed. "Sha, sha!"

The waxen pallor had faded. Chickadee was pale and wasted in appearance, but his eyes no longer stared vacantly. He recognized his mother and reached out for her breast, small mouth pursed in a sucking conformation.

Sweet Grass Woman looked to Sam for approval. He nodded. "If he wants it—certainly!"

Sweet Grass Woman bared her breast—*round again,* Sam thought, *very round, good things are round*—and nursed. Too weak to continue, the small head finally lolled and his eyes closed. That night the child slept soundly. He did not wake to toss and fret as he had done for so long.

"What?" Sam signed to Big Throat. He pointed to the tin cup, made grinding motions, pantomimed drinking.

The old woman grinned a toothless grin. *"Shi shin o wuts!"*

"Eh?"

She repeated the words, slowly and with emphasis.

"Oh!" he muttered. Shi shin meant rattlesnake. But what did the medicine have to do with rattlesnakes?

By signs Big Throat made him know the green medicine was used to draw out poison from rattlesnake bites. Shi shin o wuts was drawing poisons from the small body as it sucked out the venom also of shi shin, the rattlesnake.

"Shi shin o wuts!" he said, pleased. "Someday you've got to show me where to find the plant, how to prepare it!" Big Throat, not understanding the English words, only stared at him. Finally he gave up, kissing her cheek instead. It pleased her and seemed to some extent to allay her fear of the curse which lay on him. Chickadee, it appeared, might yet live!

With frequent dosings of the shi shin o wuts medicine, Chickadee continued to improve. Soon he was crawling about the lodge, though somewhat wobbly, dragging the immobile leg and foot after him. Soon, Sam knew the final test would come. He would remove the crude cast, the splints and bindings, and know whether the surgery had been a success. Perhaps his life was not now at stake, but his professional reputation certainly was.

Sitting at the doorway of the lodge, the child in his lap, he looked out on a sunny winter day. Sweet Grass Woman was mending a rip in his shirt. Big Throat heated stones in the fire, preparing to drop them into a hide pouch filled with water and bones to make broth for Chickadee. It was "stone boiling," the old way of cooking before the Sioux had iron pots. Big Throat liked old ways better. Chickadee gurgled and burbled, pulling at Sam's beard, now long and uncut. In a society of clean-shaven males, he was an anomaly. Absently he rolled his head aside to escape a too-vigorous yank. Something about the atmosphere of the camp puzzled him. The last few days there had been many visits of emissaries from other villages, visits unusual now that the snow was so deep and traveling difficult. The men went about grim-faced, with little of the customary joking and chaffing.

"What is it?" he asked Sweet Grass Woman. "Why?"

She did not know. That was male business and did not concern her. Soon the camp herald, Turkey Leg, would put on his prized blue forage cap and ride about, giving the news; then they would know. In the meantime, she was not concerned.

"But—"

Big Throat interrupted, pointing to Chickadee and signing that the child's broth was ready. Sam gave the child over to her and stood for a long time at the open doorflap. The tension could almost be felt. Were The People With Hats planning an attack on the Oglalas? Or were the allies—the Miniconjou, the Brulés, the Hunkpapas, the rest of the Sioux tribes—planning a surprise action of their own?

Dancer did not know either. Sam stared at the proud scrawl on a scrap of paper: *My Name Is Dancer.* "Sha, sha," he said, "Very good! William Shakespeare's reputation is in danger."

Dancer did not understand his little joke. Sam wished for the sound of English again, someone to talk to, joke with, exchange reminiscences. "Shake—shake—peer?" Dancer asked, puzzled. "Who?"

"A great writer," Sam said. "Damn near as good as you, friend!" Struggling in the unfamiliar language, supplementing his question with the *wibluta,* he asked, "Why are the people so—so—" His vocabulary ran out. But Dancer appeared to know what he meant. *Fight,* he signed, palms in front of his body and passing one before the other quickly in an alternating fashion: *rubbing out.*

"Fighting? Who?"

Dancer knew no more, or did not want to talk about it. He signed *finished* and went on making his letters with a stub of charcoal on a flat stone.

Growler was no more communicative. He had, it seemed, just been nominated for membership in the exclusive Bad Faces Society. Now he was busy trying on clothes for the occasion, proud as a newly elected alderman. He had no time to talk to Sam Blair.

"All right!" Sam blurted, exasperated. "The hell with it!"

Several weeks had now passed since the surgery on Chickadee's foot. Sam figured it was time to remove the makeshift cast and see what progress, if any, had been made. He was not anxious to make a public show of the event and told only Sweet Grass Woman of his intent. But when he got out his scissors to undo the splints and wrappings, he found the lodge suddenly, miraculously, filled with spectators. Growler was there, in his fancy togs for the Bad Faces initiation ceremony. Dancer came. Old Big Throat was already present—she was never far from her godchild—and had invited relatives. At the last moment Left Hand himself stalked in, followed by a glowering Bird Talker and a retinue from the warrior societies. Others crowded the doorway, peering.

"This had better be good," Sam murmured. Sweet Grass Woman looked puzzled. "You—say?" she asked, using the few words of English he had taught her.

"No matter," Sam said. "Nothing! It is nothing!"

Really, it was a great deal. While the Oglalas seemed to respect his medicine, they were still mercurial, unpredictable. Also, he had powerful enemies in the village. If surgery had failed, there were those who would make capital of it.

Gingerly he cut the wrappings, peeled away the splints, uncovered the long incision. Pleased with what he saw, he nodded. The cicatrice was healthy with new flesh; there was no suppuration.

"So far, so good," he told himself.

Chickadee lay quietly, trustingly, staring with button-bright eyes. Sam took the foot in his hands, moved it. Chickadee winced but did not cry out. *Indians,* Sam thought. *Indians don't show pain.* Even a child seemed to know that.

Gently he moved the foot and ankle again, testing it to its limits. It rotated as it had not before, resisting his pressure only slightly. "That's a good boy," he said. He picked Chickadee up in his arms, speaking softly.

"Now," he said, "you're going to walk, small friend."

Carefully he set the child upright, supporting him under the arms. "Put some weight on that foot," he instructed. Chickadee did not understand, but Sweet Grass Woman, coming to Sam's aid, spoke to the child.

"*Hopo!*" Sam added in one of his few Sioux words. *I am ready, let's go, what are we waiting for?*

Chickadee, fingers in mouth, grinned at him. Uncertainly he thrust out the questionable leg, propped himself on it for a moment, then stared at Sam.

"*Hopo!*" Sam repeated. Though Sweet Grass Woman drew in her breath sharply, he pushed the child forward. "*Hopo!*"

Chickadee toppled, almost fell; at the last moment he took another halting step. His face became frightened and he started to wail. But Sam was adamant.

"You can do it!" he cried. "Try, damn it!"

Again he urged Chickadee forward. This time the child took two or three faltering steps on the repaired foot. Surprised himself,

Chickadee stopped, wide-legged, and looked back at Sam and his mother.

"You walked!" Sam shouted. "There! See that, everyone?"

Grinning, Chickadee tottered about the circle of intent faces, holding arms wide for balance, experiencing for the first time an approximation to normal gait. Reeling over to Left Hand, he stared upward, fingers in mouth, gurgling. Bird Talker, scowling, turned his face away. Old Big Throat was crying, and Dancer's face was awestruck. The men from the warrior societies, lead by Growler, started a deep-voiced chant of "Hau! Hau! Hau!" to express their approval.

After a while Chickadee started to tire. Hurrying to his mother he began to cry, showing her where his foot hurt. "That's to be expected," Sam explained. "He's never walked on that foot before! It's no surprise it's beginning to hurt!" Growler translated to the spectators. "But," Sam concluded, "the foot will get stronger every day. It may not be capable of full movement, but the boy can play at blindman's buff with the other children!"

Happily they crowded around Sam Blair, laughing and shaking his hand. Growler, too, basked in Sam's reflected glory. He ran about buttonholing people, chattering, shaking hands also. Had he not been the one who brought Sam Blair to the Oglala village? Sam, watching his antics, was amused. If Growler had had a box of cigars, he would have been pressing them on the men like a ward boss in Chicago, and kissing the ladies.

"I am glad," Sweet Grass Woman signed. Then, the gesture insufficient to demonstrate her joy, she kissed his hand.

Uneasy, he pulled it away. "Here, here!" he muttered. "None of that, now!"

Tired and happy, he finally collapsed on a robe while the Oglalas filed out, chattering like magpies. Of course the repaired foot would be stiff and boardlike but it would be sufficient for Chickadee to romp and play, and not likely to cause further pain. It was a long time before Sam realized a further benefit had accrued, one that benefited him, Sam Blair, personally. He was now a personal friend of the Oglalas. No longer need he fear vengeance.

He became a respected citizen of Left Hand's village, a good-luck man, in their words. People brought him presents: a prized

Green River knife; a beaded shirt with trailing fringes along the sleeves, chest decorated with rows of dyed porcupine quills; choice cuts of meat; their own private medicine in leather sacks to be blessed by the great man. Growler, Sam suspected, was promoting much of this, as an astute manager promotes the fortunes of a political candidate. Growler was a rascal but an engaging one. Still, Sam's new status bothered him. Wishing he had someone to talk to, someone to understand his dilemma, he wrote in his journal:

> I am quite uncertain in my mind as to the Course of Action I have taken, or Rather that has been forced on me by Circumstance. Here I am, quite Comfortable in a hostile Indian Camp, friends with Savages who would not Hesitate to rape and burn and pillage in the white Settlements along the River. Moreover, I find Myself liking these People, and beginning to understand why they are Fierce in their defense of their Lands. Not only that, but I have operated on a crippled Indian child, a Boy, and restored his Locomotion. Someday he can be a Great Warrior and kill my countrymen, perhaps even some of my Friends. I am Bedevilled by the Possible consequences of what I am doing. Yet How was I to do Differently?

For a long time he sat before the fire, listening to the wind ripple the thin-scraped skins that were the boundary between him and winter. Worn out from ceaseless excursions about the circumference of the lodge, Chickadee slept. Soon, Sam promised, the child could go out in the snow and play with the other children—foot and leg, however, still protected with a splint. Sweet Grass Woman sat near Sam, sewing. *Clara*, he thought suddenly. *Clara Freeman!* For the first time he had not started an entry in his journal with *Dear Clara*. Had he already forgotten her?

To dispel morbid thoughts, he rose, stretching his arms and yawning. A sudden and welcome thought came to him. "This," he told Sweet Grass Woman, "is probably the Christmas season! I forgot all about it!"

She gazed at him, not understanding.

"It's too complicated to explain," he said, "but white people have a big celebration around this time. Mince pies and presents and a Christmas tree—" His voice trailed off as he remembered childhood

Christmases in Springfield; an orange in the toe of his stocking, the iron-runnered sled painted red and gold his father made for him, baked beans in place of the goose they could not afford.

It was already late afternoon, but he picked up a hatchet one of Big Throat's relatives had presented to him and in his new beaded shirt dashed outside. In the failing light he floundered through snow to the trees surrounding the village. Selecting a small pine with a beautiful conformation, he hacked at the trunk, finally twisting it loose from its base.

"There!" he said. "That'll do nicely!"

Hearing a strange noise, he paused. The village lay silent in the snow, tipis glowing from within by the light of cooking fires. But there was the noise again, a kind of dull thudding. Echoes from his chopping? No, that could hardly be. Still—

Bemused, he picked up the tree and started to drag it across the snow to his lodge. Again he heard the strange noise, and behind it a kind of shrill keening. Baffled, he paused knee-deep in the snow, hand cupping his ear.

Suddenly he knew the source of the strange sounds: The People With Hats! From the cover of the trees at the edge of the village galloped mounted soldiers. As they rode, they shouted, waving sabers and shooting at random. Like bears in their fur overcoats and fur caps, they charged Left Hand's camp, yelling in victory. They had surprised the somnolent village, the Sioux village that thought itself safe, deep in winter snows!

"No!" Sam screamed. Dropping the Christmas tree, he ran toward the cavalrymen, holding out hands in supplication. "Stop! Stop it!" A vision of Sweet Grass Woman sewing, Chickadee sleeping, flashed through his confused mind. However it happened, the tipi was his household. To alarm the camp, he cupped his hands to his mouth and shouted, *"Nutska we hoo!"* The words meant *white men.*

People scurried from the tipis, milling about. Warriors grabbed rifles, lances, any weapon they could find, and ran naked into the snow. The first rush of the soldiers carried them through the village and beyond; the headlong assault bowled over lodges, trampled fleeing women and children, set the ponies in the corral into a frenzy of whinnying and stamping and kicking. Sam Blair reeled back as a trooper on a big black rode him down, the shoulder of the catapulting animal knocking him spinning into the snow.

Stunned, he staggered erect, searching for his own lodge. He must get there, protect Sweet Grass Woman and Chickadee! But as he stumbled toward home, what had been home, a burst of flame and smoke erupted in his face. The soldiers were burning the lodges. Like furry dark animals they raced about, putting the torch to everything. An Oglala brave wrested a brand from the hand of a trooper; a soldier shot him from behind. All was confusion and shouting, smoke and flame. Somewhere the blaze reached an ammunition box. Exploding cartridges showered in all directions, wounding friend and foe alike.

"Stop it!" Sam sobbed, grappling with a trooper who was running his saber through a wriggling youth on the crusted snow; the blood stained dark on the icy whiteness. He twisted the saber from the man's hand and raised it, poising it above his head. Then realization overcame him. He could not kill a white man, even one intent on Sam's own death. He would have died if Dancer had not knocked him aside and run the trooper through with his lance.

"Friend, come!" Dancer urged, gasping for breath. "Come away to the trees! We will fight them from there! There are so many of them!"

Transfixed, Sam stood spraddle-legged in the snow, surrounded by death and destruction.

"Come!" Dancer called. "Friend, come!"

Sam stood rooted in his tracks, fumbling a hand over his brow. "Stop," he repeated, wearily. "Please, stop!" He was caught in the vortex of a whirlwind. Around him men fought, whooped, screamed, died, against a background of burning lodges. Smoke stung his eyes. He was weeping, but not from the smoke. Out of the drifting vapors a horse loomed high and powerful, eyes rolling whitely. A furry mounted soldier aimed a carbine at him. Almost as in a dream Sam saw the wild-eyed black horse bear down on him. The trooper bent in the saddle, riding like a centaur, arms extending the deadly weapon toward him.

"No!" Sam protested, almost quietly. He turned away, not wanting to look. As he did so a flower of orange flame bloomed in his face. At the borders of that deadly flower he saw the face of the rider. It was—there could be no doubt—it was Luther Speck, the young corporal Sam had treated for the scabies in his office at Fitch's Landing. Speck, Luther Speck—the young man whom Sam had helped fill out the Government forms for Luther's mother to receive a pension. Luther Speck! As Sam fell, his eyes were fixed on Luther's white face. Luther knew, too, whom he had shot down in Left Hand's hostile village.

CHAPTER 6

For a long time he wandered through a terrible dream, seeing a once-familiar landscape dotted now with skeleton-like burned tipis and sprawled lifeless bodies, smelling smoke and blood and the acrid stench of black powder. At times he seemed to wake, calling out in panic for a familiar face, a familiar voice, but strong arms pressed him down. He slept again, this time without dreaming. And one day he woke again to life, everything suddenly sharp and clear in his vision.

Sweet Grass Woman bent over her sewing. The open doorflap framed a triangle of cold light. The lodge was warm; a small fire smoldered. "I see you," he murmured. "You are here."

Quickly she came to him, a light in her eyes. "Yes. I am here. And you have come back."

"Have I—" Remembering, he supplemented his halting Sioux with signs. *Have I been away a long time?*

Yes.

Where are the people? Where is Growler? Suddenly the memory of the battle came to him. It came fast, flooding in on him, overwhelming him. Christmas, the tree—then the distant sound of hooves, the rattle of gunfire, wild yelling of Major Henry Cushing's troopers as they attacked the camp, Left Hand's sleeping camp. The horrible vision swamped his being, filled his eyes and ears and nose and mouth, pushed him back toward the nightmare in which he had wandered so long. He screamed at the troopers, shook his fist, swore. When his chest, feeling so strange, started to hurt him, he paused, passion abated. Sweet Grass Woman put her cheek against his and stroked his face.

"Where are the people?" he asked. "Where is Growler? Where is Dancer?"

Growler is dead. Killed by the soldiers.

Growler dead? Dead, the man who had brought Sam Blair to Left Hand's camp; the Oglala politician who had become his friend and proud new member of the Bad Faces? He felt a keen sense of loss. Growler had been a self-serving rascal, but Sam liked him. Life would hardly be the same without pockmarked Growler.

"Dancer?" He had seen Dancer, as if in a dream, though.

He was hurt, but is all right now.

"Chickadee?"

She called. The child came trotting like a small pony. Chickadee limped, yet he walked. Sam pulled the boy to him, kissed him in the gesture Sweet Grass Woman found strange, yet delightful.

"The—the soldiers?"

We fought them. They burned the village, spoiled our food, hurt and killed a lot of the people. But we drove them away and killed a lot of them too.

For the first time he was aware of a mossy poultice on his chest, fastened by bands of precious cloth. He looked down, felt it wonderingly.

The soldiers shot you in the chest. You were sick for a long time and talked crazy. Big Throat saved your life. She brewed herbs for you, made poultices, sat with you as much as I did, kept you clean.

Luther, Sam remembered. *Luther Speck.* Luther had shot him in the chest. He could still see Luther's amazed face. Luther was probably sorry; he was that kind of a young man.

"I owe you my life," Sam murmured, trying to find the words, the signs, to tell Sweet Grass Woman. Gesturing, he beckoned her near. Careful of his bandaged chest, Sweet Grass Woman lay close, head pillowed in the hollow between his neck and shoulder. Chickadee, jealous, limped over on fat baby legs and burrowed between them, sighing comfortably. *My Indian household!* Sam thought. It was a strange idea, both comforting and unsettling.

In the cracked mirror Sweet Grass Woman brought him, he stared at the scarecrow. Always tall and lanky, his flesh now hung in loose folds, like old and yellowed muslin. Dark eyes stared, deep in their sockets, and his cheekbones were gaunt ledges. His ribs stood out like the ivory keys on a pianoforte. The beard was long and straggling; he had to push it aside to examine the bullet hole in his chest.

Imagine! He stared wonderingly at the healing wound. The ball had hit near the left nipple, apparently grazing the lung and missing the heart. Perhaps it passed through the narrow space between kidney and duodenum and then lodged spent, after its downward passage, in the muscles of his back. He could find no exit wound; bad ammunition, probably—there had been unscrupulous profiteers in the war. Now they were busy selling defective cartridges to the War Department. Well, he was lucky to be alive.

"What month is this?" he asked.

She told him it was The Moon When The Raccoons Come Out. At first he did not understand. By repeated questioning he finally decided it was February. If it had indeed been around Christmas when he was wounded, then he had lain in the tipi, near death, for weeks! A month or more had gone from his life. Yet he lived. He was grateful for that and for the loving care that made it possible.

He wrote again in his journal:

Because I roused the Camp against the soldiers, and was wounded in the fighting, the People have made me an Honorary Member of the Society called the Strong Hearts and given me back the Starr Revolver they took from me. The Initiation Ceremony was Impressive. A book could be written about their religion, their ceremonies, their Way of Life. The Strong Hearts are able to handle Hot Coals without being burned. They pass them around from hand to Hand, even walk on them without being Burned. I think, however, there is a Trick to it. I saw a man rubbing his hands with the juice of what old Big Throat calls *is se wa nots*. It is what I have heard called Purple Cone Flower back in Illinois. Anyway this Juice seems to protect them from burns. After that they Danced a lot and made me join the Ring also. Finally they put on my Head a bonnet of Crow Feathers, very Fine, and gave me the name of Lightning Man, probably because of the Perkins Magnetic Tractors I used on old Bird Talker when I first arrived here. Then we all Smoked, the Mixture of shaved Bark and strong Tobacco they use made my head Swim. I am now a Strong

Heart, though Honorary, and am permitted to Sit In on their Meetings, although not allowed of Course to Speak nor Vote.

Bird Talker, the shaman, reluctantly became Sam's friend. Now that his rival Growler was out of the way, he could afford to be magnanimous. "Growler was a fool," the old man said, "but now he has gone up the Starry Way." After the meeting, he put a kind of amulet around Sam's neck—a polished gemlike stone incised with mystical signs, hanging from a rawhide cord.

"Friends," he said. "You. Me." He touched the stone with a trembling finger. "When I joined the Strong Hearts I did a lot of brave things, so they gave it to me." He sighed. "Now I am too old to fight anymore, so it is for you, Lightning Man." He made the *lightning* sign: in homage to Sam's Electrical Tractors his index finger described the jagged path of the electrical flash.

"Hie," Sam said in thanks. "Hie, hie." He put the worn and greasy cord about his neck and shook hands.

"It is beautiful—sha, sha!" They became friends, Bird Talker now referring more difficult cases to Lightning Man, his copractitioner.

Stronger now, Sam went out to walk. Helped by other tribes of the Sioux nation, angry and resentful at the treacherous winter attack of the horse soldiers, Left Hand was directing the rebuilding of his village. New lodgepoles were cut. The Miniconjou brought spare hides to stretch over them. Some Cheyenne friends supplied dried corn and beans traded from the Rees, and a Brulé deputation that had ambushed an Army supply train provided much black powder and ball, along with metallic cartridges for the newer repeating rifles. Along with their gifts, the allies brought savage and eloquent oratory. Sam, permitted to sit at the periphery of Left Hand's great lodge, listened, chin in hand, to Gall, Two Moons, Dull Knife, other great chieftains.

This land is our land! These white people, The People With Hats, are trying to drive us out. They want us to leave our sacred mountain, the burial ground of our fathers! They want to dig up the land and plant things, make holes in the earth to look for gold, tell us where we can hunt and where we have got to stay away.

The orator raised hands over his head in a ritual plea toward Wakan Tanka, the Great One.

Friends, how long will this go on? We were here first! The Gods
gave us this land! The People With Hats did not ask us to come in
here. They just came. But we belong here. This earth is our mother.
The rivers are our blood. The sky is our breath!

Sam had trouble following the words, but the gestures were
clear.

When the grass is green, all of us should get together and drive
them out! That is what Wakan Tanka wants! It is up to us to de-
fend our Mother, the earth!

There was a deep chorus of "Hau, hau, hau!" Sam, caught up in
the eloquence, joined in. Then, guiltily, he fell silent, glancing
around to see if anyone had observed him. Had he become an Indian? The thought chilled him. How could he, a white man, en-
dorse a Sioux campaign against his neighbors—people like the
Freemans, Jacob Almayer, Ma Bidwell, Charlie Daigle who ran the
livery stable in Fitch's Landing, Bertha Rambouillet and her girls?
Yet the beleaguered Sioux had a case.

Ill at ease, he trudged through melting snow to visit an old man
in trouble with his bowels. Sam gave the ancient a dose of his rapidly disappearing calomel, and refused a cut of frozen meat in
thanks. The man's wife, nevertheless, knelt before him and pressed
his hand to her withered cheek.

"Here, here!" he said, embarrassed. "That's not necessary!"

Even when he was leaving the tipi the old woman clung to his
hand. She stood waving for a long time after he left. In a way, she
reminded him of Mrs. Freeman, Clara's mother—silvery hair in
braids, wrinkled kindly face, even the gingham dress, though the
long deerhide moccasins, beaded in bright designs, gave a garish
touch to the ensemble. *People*, he thought. *We are all just people.*

Carrying the physician's satchel, he was about to enter his own
lodge when he heard a commotion at the far edge of the village,
near the cleft in the great ledge where the troopers from Fort Pike
had broken through to attack Left Hand's village. But this was no
attack. Laughing and shouting, the Oglalas ran to greet a visitor.
The winter-thin ponies in their corral whickered joyously, kicking
up their heels.

Down the rubbled slope a packtrain picked its way—a rider on a
speckled paint, and a file of heavy-laden mules. The rider was

Cletus Wiley, in the same odorous buckskins he had worn ever since Sam had known him. Grinning toothlessly, the old man dug into a tattered pocket and brought out handfuls of hard sugar candies which he flung to the children. Cletus was apparently an old friend. They pulled White Whiskers from the saddle and clustered around, chattering and laughing, shaking his hand, slapping him on the back.

I bring blankets, he signed, speaking also in the sibilant Sioux tongue. *I hear you lost blankets in the fight with the horse soldiers!*

Like children the women ransacked the pack mules, laughing and giggling. The mules, never easy with Indians, pawed the earth and laid their ears back. The men of the tribe, more dignified, gave Cletus a pipe to smoke and squatted with him on a sun-warmed ledge to exchange gossip.

"Cletus!" Sam called.

In midspeech the old man bit off a word, hands paused in midair.

"It's me, Cletus!"

The old man stared at Sam, standing in the snow with the black satchel hanging from his hand.

"It's me, Cletus—Sam Blair!"

Cletus' jaw dropped open. He blinked, squinted. "Sam? Sam Blair?"

"That's right."

"But you—you was supposed to be dead, Doc! The hostiles killed your old Thelma horse, burned the trap—"

"They didn't kill me," Sam explained. "They brought me up here, thinking I had some kind of magic, I guess. When they found out I didn't, they were about to kill me." He grinned at Cletus. "You remember those Magnetic Tractors?"

Cletus grinned also. "Greatest invention since corn whisky!" He licked his lips. "Didn't bring 'em with you, did you?"

"I used them," Sam said, "to give quite a treatment to Bird Talker, the medicine man. That impressed them, and so they spared me."

"Well, I never!" Cletus stood back and stared. "By crikey, you sure changed some, though! You ain't never had much meat on your bones, but you look like a skellington, you sure do!"

"In the fighting," Sam explained, "I got a ball in the chest. I was lucky, though. I survived."

That night the Oglalas laid on a feast for White Whiskers. Though supplies were scarce, they roasted meat, boiled Indian turnips, and were lavish with the sugar and tea Cletus brought. Afterward they smoked his tobacco, closing their eyes in sensual delight at the taste, the aroma, of pure tobacco without *kinnikinnick*, the willow-bark shavings they often used to stretch their store of white man's tobacco.

Afterward, Cletus and Sam sat together around the fire in Sam's tipi. Sweet Grass Woman and Chickadee slept on a robe away from the circle of firelight.

"Looks like you're pretty well settled in here, Doc," Cletus observed.

"I guess so."

"They tell me you tried to escape onct, right after old Growler latched on to you."

Sam's toes still ached occasionally from that freezing night atop the Chetish.

"Yes," he admitted, "but Growler brought me back."

Cletus lit his pipe. "Growler was a fine old coon. He'd 'a made a good U.S. congressman."

"You know," Sam said, "in a way I'm glad Growler brought me back. I practice medicine here, good medicine, and help a lot of people. That's what a doctor is supposed to do, isn't he?"

Cletus grinned slyly. "Got you an Indian woman too, I see!"

"Yes."

"Best kind! Don't never sass you, always takes good care of you, makes good mothers. You might of done worse, pilgrim. I guess you know you're already a might big bear round these parts. The Oglalas figger you're good luck." For a while he puffed on his pipe. "Me—I was just on my way to a Ree village where I got me a nice fat lady. Stopped by to leave off the blankets and stuff."

"*Another* woman? How many have you got?"

Cletus knocked dottle from his pipe. "A few! I keep 'em sprinkled round the country so I don't never have to go far to get my ashes hauled." Suddenly he brightened. "You mentioned them Tractors! Got 'em here?"

"Yes, they're in that hide chest, the one with the designs painted on it."

"'Cause I got to have me a session before I see my Ree woman," Cletus explained. "Been feelin' a mite poorly of late. I need my giblets sparked up. You remember that time in Fitch's Landing you gave me a treatment? That time I stayed at Bertha Rambouillet's house all day?"

"All right, all right!" Sam laughed. "We'll see what we can do for your giblets before you leave!" More seriously, he said, "Weren't you on Major Cushing's payroll as a civilian scout for the cavalry at Fort Pike?"

"Was!" the old man snorted. He spat into the fire. For a long moment he was silent. They could hear a trickling of water about the lodge. The snow was melting; it might be an early spring. "I quit when Cushing and Andy Wyatt planned to bushwhack old Left Hand and his people in their winter camp. The major and me had words. Andy bawled me out too. But I wasn't about to lead no soldiers up the Chetish for a sneaky trick like that! So I quit, just before I got fired."

Cletus hesitated for a moment. "Andy and Clara Freeman got married at the post in November. Military wedding, with crossed swords and all that fooforaw. Anyway, her and Andy went to Washington. He got hisself a tour of duty at the War Department in Washington. Andy's pa is some big bug in an iron foundry there, made millions during the war. The word is around Pa Wyatt bought a big house for the two of 'em somewhere near the Capitol."

Clara and Andy Wyatt! Sam had known it was going to happen, yet the news of the big house in Washington put a seal of finality on it. Speaking carefully, he asked, "Does anyone know I'm up here, in Left Hand's camp? I mean—"

"I heard it noised round," Cletus said. "I guess someone seen you when they hit the camp. Leastwise, that was the rumor."

Sam's heart sank. He wet his lips, trying to think of a way to garner additional information. Cletus went on, poking at the fire.

"I don't like the look of things. The pot is comin' to a boil. Left Hand and Gall and Two Moons and the rest ain't likely to let Cushing's raid pass without no notice. I daresay, right now the tribes are planning a big fight of some kind—a gravy stirrin' is what they call it."

"I hope not," Sam said. "There's been too much blood shed already. Still—" He told the old man about the frequent visits of the allies, their long councils, the fiery oratory. "I guess it can't be avoided. There's bad blood on both sides."

"I hear," Cletus went on, "that come spring the War Department aims to settle the Sioux's hash for once and for all. There's talk of one big final push. Crook's to come up from the south, Terry from the north, and Custer west from Fort Lincoln to cap the jug."

"Custer?" Sam remembered General Custer at Five Forks, during the war, when the general was breveted for gallantry. Custer looked like a circus rider gone mad, with his hussar jacket and tight velvet pants trimmed in dirty gold lace. Since the war, Custer's devil-may-care style, so effective at Yellow Tavern, Winchester, and Fisher's Hill, had gotten him into trouble.

"Custer," Cletus confirmed. "The Sioux call him Pa Huska—Long Hair." He got up, uneasy. "Maybe I'm talkin' out of school! But I'd advise you to get the hell out of here, Sam. Go back to Springfield or wherever before the lid blows off the pot!"

Before the old man's departure next day, Sam cranked up the Magnetic Tractors and gave him a "treatment." He was afraid the voltaic level from the magneto was too much, but Cletus hung doggedly to the polished electrodes, squealing in mingled pleasure and pain, urging Sam to crank faster. Finally Sam's arm tired. He dropped the wooden handle. Cletus collapsed on a buffalo robe. Sweet Grass Woman, frightened, ran to Cletus but he waved her off.

"'M all right!" he protested, his tongue thick. "Perfectly all right, ma'am! Just"—he gasped—"jush give me a minute to get my wind back!" After a while he sat up and took a cup of tea. His eyes were bright and conversation animated. "I feel like I could take on a treeful of catamounts, yes, I do! I'm a leaping trout of the waters, a Goddamned snapping turtle with bear's claws, alligator teeth, and the devil's tail! I'm a hoss that was never rode, and I can grin like a hyena till I peel the bark right off a log! Waaaagh!"

Sam, winding up the electrical cords, said anxiously, "Now, Cletus, don't overdo yourself!"

The old man wiped his whiskered mouth. The straggly hairs on his dome seemed to stand up as though also revivified. "Oh, won't my Ree woman be happy! It'll be like Christmas and New Year's and the Fourth of July all rolled into one!"

The next morning Cletus sat his paint pony in the rain, unladen pack mules tethered behind him to a long rope. In the wet meadow the Oglalas gathered to say farewell to their friend. Left Hand himself attended, with Bird Talker and leaders to the warrior societies. Sweet Grass Woman stood beside Sam, Chickadee in her arms.

"Good-by, Doc," Cletus said, sticking out his hand. "And good luck, whatever you do!"

Sam grasped the hand warmly. "I'll remember your advice!" he promised. "Cletus, I'll remember you, too, even if we never see each other again. You were a good friend!"

Cletus waved in salute. The little packtrain filed away in the misty rain, climbing toward the gap in the ridge. Sam and Sweet Grass Woman and Chickadee went back to the lodge.

That night he lay for a long time thinking, hands clasped behind his head. Concerned, Sweet Grass Woman tried to find out what troubled him, but he could not find the words to explain. Even so, his thoughts were not clear in his own mind. *Get out before the lid blows off the pot!* But where? Back to Fitch's Landing? Certainly not; he was probably *persona non grata* there. People would never forgive his throwing in with Indians. Springfield? Sam had been gone from there a long time, he owed a lot of bills, hardly would know anyone in town. Most likely Pa was dead, and Ma too, by now.

Sensing his dilemma, Sweet Grass Woman lay close and tried to comfort him. Their bodies pressed together, his hand strayed over her stomach. It was then he knew, for the first time, that Sweet Grass Woman was pregnant with his, Sam Blair's, child.

CHAPTER 7

The Red River had been formed in Dakota Territory by the union of the Bois de Sioux and the Ottertail. That area was fertile, and a number of half-breeds of mixed French and Indian blood lived there as farmers and traders. The Oglalas called them the *slota,* or "grease people," because of the grease the half-breeds used to lubricate the wheels of their big carts. The Sioux and the Cheyennes were friendly with the slota, respecting their mixed blood. The combination of ancestry, the Indians thought, gave the Red River people understanding of both white and red men. Consequently, the slota were considered valuable go-betweens in trouble between the Indians and the whites.

Louis Jean Baptiste Moreau was welcomed when on a snowy March day he came to visit Left Hand's village. This time, however, the half-breed was not on a trading expedition. He smoked with Left Hand and the heads of the warrior societies, then produced a paper from the General Commanding the Department of the Missouri, complete with wax seal and red ribbon. All Sioux and Cheyennes, the paper said, were to leave their villages and come in at once to Standing Rock Reservation, or soldiers would be sent to fetch them.

Left Hand was astonished and angry. The Standing Rock reservation was on the Missouri, almost two hundred and fifty miles to the east. Not only that; spring was coming. The Oglalas were anxious to prepare for the annual buffalo hunt. Anyway, what right did Star Shoulder Man have to tell them where to go, summon them like children?

Angrily the chief pulled off his breech clout and contemptuously displayed his genitals. "I am a man!" he howled. "We are all men here! Why should we come running when that Star Shoulder Man snaps his fingers and whistles? Dogs act like that—not Sioux!"

Moreau was apologetic; he had only been hired to deliver the order. Noncommittal, he shook hands with everyone, leaving the document. As soon as Moreau departed, Left Hand tore it into bits and dropped it into the fire.

"We touched the pen with them!" he protested. "They told us all this land"—he spread his arms wide—"this land was ours! They promised to let us live here for all time, to hunt buffalo and raise our children and bury the dead and be good children of Wakan Tanka! Standing Rock? That place?" He spat. "That place is a jail! No Sioux will ever live in a jail!"

"Hau, hau!" everyone applauded, and the matter was forgotten as another piece of white man's insolence. Reservations, indeed!

Sam, allowed to sit in a remote corner of the great lodge, was fascinated by the oratory, but disturbed. Steam was certainly building. The rumor was spreading that the Miniconjou and the Brulés and the Sans Arcs and their Cheyenne allies were getting ready for a great conclave, somewhere to the north, to decide on a unified plan—as unified as any Indian plan could be—to beat back the tide of white men. But he certainly did not want to be caught in such a conflagration. Still, would the Oglalas let him depart? Not yet entirely recovered from his wound, *could* he go? Could he manage the trip to some outpost of civilization—Bozeman, perhaps, or Virginia City? Doctors were probably scarce there. He might prosper in a new scene.

Uncertain, he dawdled. With the coming of spring, life grew more pleasant in the village. Sweet Grass Woman was loving and tender; Chickadee daily grew stronger and more active, though the mended foot would always be stiff. Too, Sam had many good friends in the camp. Dancer was becoming almost fluent in English, and Sam now had a flourishing practice with varied cases of kidney trouble, heart disease, and liver complaint, along with an occasional mashed finger or broken leg. *Tomorrow,* he vowed, *I will ask to speak with Left Hand and see if he will give me horses and supplies and let me leave his village.* But Left Hand was busy with councils of war and visiting emissaries, and Sam was busy too. Time passed.

"It is The Moon When Corn Is Planted," he wrote in his journal late one night, coming from the tipi of a woman who had trouble birthing her baby—a fat and healthy little rascal, once Sam had him turned and pointing in the right direction. "Of course, the Oglalas do not Plant Corn. That is not a thing for a Warrior to do. But the Rees plant corn and trade Corn and Beans and Squash to the Sioux."

The Moon When Corn Is Planted. He chewed on a precious stub of pencil. May? June? He did not know how the Sioux calendar corresponded with that of the white men. But the weather was warming. While there were occasional blustery days, even snow squalls, spring had already arrived. Summer could not be far behind. Had he been here, in this Sioux village for, rapidly he calculated, six, possibly seven months? Yes, it was possible. Shaking his head at the thought, he continued to write:

> Before long that little Boy I delivered will be a member of one of the junior Societies—the Foxes, Badgers, or Rabbits. The Oglalas start them young to learn the ways of the Warrior—throwing lances at a Tree, stalking each other as Enemies, or learning to break a Fraxious Colt. From Infancy they are trained to Hunt and Fight. That is what a Man is expected to do.

For some reason a fit of depression came on him. He threw down the pencil, closed the journal. His mood was not helped when Dancer came in and squatted, ready for another English lesson. The young man instantly divined his mood; Dancer was a sensitive youth.

"Sad?" Dancer made the sign: *Heart laid on the ground.*

Sam nodded.

"Why?"

"I don't know."

"Well," Dancer said, "I am not sad. I am happy!" He went on, in a mix of hand language, English, and Sioux. "Soon there will be a lot of fighting. That is good! That is what a man needs in the summer—fighting! After sitting a long time in camp, it is good to go out and fight. We fight the Crows every summer. The Sioux and the Crows have been enemies for a long time." Dancer stretched his hands apart to show the passage of years. "In our Winter Calendar that Bird Talker keeps, it shows us fighting with the Crows as far back as anyone can remember. But this summer we are going to fight The People With Hats, too!"

Sam's eyes narrowed; he felt suddenly annoyed.

"It is the truth," Dancer confirmed, mistaking Sam's silence for doubt. "I heard it from a man who is Drum Keeper for the Bad Faces!"

Sam stared into the dying fire. He had good friends on both sides.

"I had a dream last night," Dancer continued. He closed his eyes, reliving his vision. "I will die up there, somewhere—" He gestured toward the north. "I am to count *coup* three times, and everyone will see I am a good fighter. Then someone will kill me." He was rapt in the dream. "Then I will ride up the Starry Road and be remembered among the people as a great warrior!" Proudly he beamed at Sam, expecting approval.

"You're a fool!" Sam snorted in English.

Puzzled at the strange word, Dancer frowned. "Foo—fool?"

"Yes, a fool! A Goddamned fool!"

Dancer still did not understand the word, but he understood Sam's anger. He grew irate himself.

"What is wrong with you?"

"Nothing's the matter with me!" Sam shouted. "It's you—people like you stupid people—people like Major Cushing at Fort Pike and the damned U. S. Congress and the Indian Bureau and all the rest of the fools!"

Uncertain, lips set tight, Dancer grasped the haft of his knife. "You talk crazy!" He put a fist close to his forehead, forefinger extended upward, and made a whirling motion. "Crazy!"

"What's crazy," Sam insisted, "what's *really* crazy—is to want to die when you're a fine young man with all your life before you! Damn it, friend, you've got a brain, a good brain! You could do something to stop the needless slaughter that's coming! But what do you do? You sit on your butt happy as a clam and tell me you plan to die this summer!" Agitated, he rose to pace the confines of the lodge. Sweet Grass Woman, entering with a sack of freshly dug tipsin roots, stared at him. "It's insane!" Sam shouted. "Insane, I tell you!"

Dancer was both angry and confused. "Clam? Happy as clam?" He turned to Sweet Grass Woman. "What clam? In—sane? What mean, insane?"

Helpless, Sam threw up his hands. "I'm sorry," he apologized. "I didn't mean to be angry. It was just that—that—" Words failed him. Frustrated, he held out his hand to Dancer. But the young man was offended. Angrily he stalked from Sam's lodge, abandoning the flat rock on which he usually scrawled his English assignments.

"What is wrong?" Sweet Grass Woman asked.

He sighed, rubbing his forehead. "Nothing."

"But I *know*."

She came to him, pressing close, seeking to comfort him. When he put his arms about her, he felt the growing bulge in her stomach. *A son. His son.* Even if all else were possible, could he abandon Sweet Grass Woman and the unborn child? He almost wept at the cruel dilemma.

Spring grew, skirted summer. Sam was preparing an Indian pharmacopoeia; the fat daily journal now bulged with pressed specimens of medicinal herbs employed by the Oglalas, along with extensive notes. Enthused by the scope and efficacy of their medicine, he hoped someday—he did not know where or how—to publish an authoritative volume on the subject. Even now, his own medical supplies becoming exhausted, he often used old Big Throat's herbal compounds to treat his patients.

With something approaching relief, he decided he would have to finish at least the groundwork for the pharmacopoeia before making any decision to leave Left Hand's village. In the meantime he and Big Throat prowled the vernal meadows, looking for rare plants and herbs and shrubs, accompanied by Chickadee and the other children, who thought it an exciting game. The boys and girls, apprised of his needs, stalked the plants as if they were the traditional Crow enemy, pouncing with shouts of triumph counting coup as in battle, bringing them proudly to Sam. There was *i se yo,* a tuber used to make an infusion in water, good for stomach pain. There was *ma e tse i yo,* powerful headache remedy; Sam believed it had the power to shrink swollen and throbbing blood vessels in the head. *A hyov is se e* treated the common cold. Then there were *ta si mins* and *his ta a tsi* and *mot si i un;* so many others, they made his head swim, for female disorders and lung fever and colic in infants. Busily he sketched, pressed specimens, transcribed Big Throat's comments. His journal, already replete with comments on his life with the Sioux and their ways and customs and language, grew to encyclopedia size.

One day, wandering far from the camp, the little band moved through a meadow alight with yellow daisies, mauve hyacinth blossoms, the red of clustering vetch. They brought with them dried meat for the noon meal. Big Throat found wild onions in a marsh and dug roots of the mariposa lily. They dined splendidly on vegetables stewed with the meat in an iron pot. Afterward, Big Throat and Sam sat on a grassy knoll, watching the children play. Chickadee, Sam was glad to see, kept up well with the others in spite of the stiffened foot. At times he seemed to tire, but in general Chickadee kept pace with the other Oglala urchins—running, jumping, and shouting as children do in a school playground.

Watching Sam, Big Throat seemed curious. Filling her pipe, she took a coal from the fire between horny fingers and dropped it into the charred bowl. "You think," she observed. "All the time you think." She shook her head. "It is not good for a man to think so much. Sometimes"—she took a deep draft of the smoke—"sometimes it is enough just to look." She gestured at the peaceful scene. "Just look, enjoy! That is enough."

Sam pulled up a blade of new grass. In remembrance of his own childhood, he split the blade, put it to his lips, blew. Hearing the sweet whistle, Chickadee left his play, came close. Eyes round, the boy picked his own blade of grass in imitation of Sam. Soon the rest of the children gathered round, making reedy music. The older boys soon tired, however, and chased a rabbit over a ridge with their stick lances.

"There is a dog on your back," Big Throat observed. "A black dog. It is heavy. It is pulling you down."

He was uneasy at her prescience. "There is no dog!" he muttered.

She puffed a circle of smoke. "I know that dog. When my husband died and went up the Starry Way, that dog was on me. Oh, friend—I know that dog!"

He threw the bit of grass away, almost angrily. Chickadee, uncertain at Sam's change of mood, stared at him with bright alert eyes. From beyond the ridge came a whoop as one of the boys closed on the fleeing rabbit.

"Mother, you are right," Sam finally admitted. "There is a dog, a big black dog. And he is heavy!"

The whoops became louder. A boy, running, burst over the rocky ledge and bounded toward them in great leaps, like a deer. Sam, preoccupied, watched the boy without interest. "I do not know what to do," he said to Big Throat. "Should I—should I—"

Face contorted with excitement, the running boy neared them. He was not chasing rabbits. Small belly heaving, he pulled Sam's sleeve. "*Nutska we hoo!*" he gasped. "White soldiers! The People With Hats!"

Sam ran to the ridge, stared through the screen of junipers. Below, in the valley of the rain-swollen river, lumbered a military supply train, white canvas covers bright against the green of the grass. Outriders, alert for Sioux, paralleled the path of the wagons. There was a heavy vanguard, and a body of infantry toiled in the wake of the wagons.

This was no casual supply train, bound to Fort Pike to replenish Major Henry Cushing's winter-exhausted supplies. This was a striking force, complete with wagons—even a herd of cattle—bound for the Yellowstone. Sam felt the hairs on the back of his neck prickle. He remembered Cletus Wiley's words: *Crook's to come up from the south, Gibbon from the north* . . . Though it was cool and shady in the junipers and he was in no danger from the distant column, he began to sweat. Discovering his hand on the butt of the restored Starr revolver, he drew it quickly away as if the grease-dark wood burned.

"We go back, quick!" Big Throat tugged at his sleeve. "Go back, tell the people!"

Slowly he withdrew from the junipers, thinking. One small boy, excited, broke off a switch and hurled it, like a lance, at the far-off column. Another gathered stones and flung them. They were ready to fight.

"All right," Sam agreed. "We go back."

He paused for a moment, parted the junipers again, and stared over the ledge. The column was traveling fairly fast, considering its size and length. Already the vanguard had passed into trees bordering the river. Sam felt almost relieved. He could never have caught up with them anyway.

Big Throat pulled again at his sleeve, impatient. "All right," he agreed. "Hopo! Let's go!"

When they reached camp, news of the heavily armed column had preceded them. Young Smoke Eater on his fast horse had already reported the movement to Left Hand, and the village was preparing to move, fearing to be outflanked. Strangely, a holiday mood prevailed. After the long winter, the people were eager to travel, to taste fresh buffalo meat, to ride through blossoming meadows. They did not seem to fear the soldiers very much. Bad Soup, one of Big Throat's widowed friends, helped Sam take down his lodge and pack household goods. Sweet Grass Woman, heavy with the burden of her unborn child, wrapped precious crockery cups in grass and fitted them into an ammunition box. Chickadee gathered his toys and stuffed them into a sack to be carried on a travois drawn by a camp dog.

"It is time to move anyway!" Bad Soup enthused. "I do not like to stay in one place a long time!" Wrinkled nose working, she sniffed the nimble air of spring. "It is time to ride out, to hunt, to meet old friends!"

Sam, jerking the hackamore of a rolling-eyed pony, asked, "Mother, where are we going?"

The old lady gestured northward. "Up toward the Big Broken-Back Star. With so many soldiers around, our father Left Hand says we ought to get close to our Brulé and Miniconjou and Cheyenne brothers. If there are a lot of us all together, The People With Hats will not bother us. That way we can hunt and visit and have a good time together."

Sam tightened a packrope, trying to remember the geography of the Territory. That way—north—lay the Yellowstone. Old Fort Tullock was up there, at the junction of the Yellowstone and the Big Horn. Perhaps the abandoned fort had been regarrisoned in anticipation of the Indian campaign Cletus Wiley had mentioned. Leave the Oglalas or not, he was no worse off to accompany Left Hand's village in its travels northward.

When the column finally moved out, it was a half-mile wide and several miles long. The Sioux rode casually, enjoying the fine weather. Game was plentiful—buffalo, deer, antelope. Scouts were ahead, behind, on both flanks. It was the season to hunt, to gorge on fresh meat, to savor fresh-sprouting greens. As they trudged under their burdens, women sang, chatted, visited. The men, in bright clothing, hair tied up on the forehead in warrior fashion, rode grandly. In the rear the pony herd was minded by boys of the tribe, grave with authority. It reminded Sam of his family's annual outing at Lake Nawata, near Springfield, for the Masonic picnic. Watching a child slyly pilfer pemmican from a hamper, he was reminded of his own theft of a blueberry pie long ago, so long ago.

During the morning they came on a small gathering of buffalo in a meadow. Not wasting precious ammunition, the young men surrounded the herd, galloping through it to loose a shower of arrows. Fascinated, Sam stayed behind to watch them expertly butcher the carcasses.

The operation was done with a precision and dispatch a professional meatcutter might envy. The great cow was laid on her belly with legs spread stiffly out. With a knife a long cut was made from the upper lip between the horns and along the backbone to the root of the tail. Then the outer blanket of flesh was removed from back and sides in one piece. The tongue, a choice morsel, was cut out, and the fat hump removed at the backbone. A hind leg, cactus-studded hoof used as hatchet, broke the ribs from the backbone in the form of a slab from either side.

"Sha, sha!" Sam chuckled, amused at the clever use of the animal's own hoof as a slaughtering tool.

Liver, fat, and brains were then removed and dumped in a pocket-shaped section of gut for later use in tanning hides. The paunch was turned wrong-side out and saved for the grease which would later be boiled from it. The hide, split along the belly, was used to wrap up the meat, the packages finally roped atop uneasy ponies. Small bits of meat still clinging to the hide would later be scraped off by the women. Sun-dried, they made filling snacks, and were also good to enrich soups.

Looking back, Sam could see hardly any evidence of the slaughtered animals. They had been utilized almost completely by the

Sioux hunters; anything left would soon disappear, decaying to enrich the earth so that new generations of buffalo would prosper.

That night they camped along the reverse side of a high ridge for protection against the wind. The night was powdered with stars, air fragrant with smoke and roasting meat. Sam, following Bad Soup's instructions, stuck willow shoots in a circle, bent them over and tied them in the middle, draping blankets over the framework for a temporary shelter. *June*, he wondered? It must be, though the nights at this altitude were still chilly.

All about smoldered the buffalo-chip fires of the Oglalas. People visited, chatted. Someone played on a kind of lute made from a green bough strung with gut. In a pocket below the top of the ridge the pony herd grazed, ghostly forms moving in the pallid afterglow of sunset. A cheese-yellow moon crept above the eastern hills.

After roast hump and a hoarded handful of white man's soda crackers, Sam lay down beside Sweet Grass Woman. Chickadee, face and hands smeared with hump fat, slept blissfully. One hand behind his head, Sam encircled her shoulder with his other arm. Content, she pressed close. He kissed her and she laughed, a low musical laugh. It was almost like singing—a melody.

"Are you happy?" he whispered.

Knowing his difficulties, even yet, with the language, she spoke slowly, carefully. "How should I be other?"

Watching through a rent in the encircling blanket, he saw a star slide across the gap.

"You?" she asked.

He did not answer immediately, but pulled her closer. It was as if he were unwilling to let anything, even a word, slip between them. Yet the lonely feeling remained, a small and worrisome wedge.

"You?" she repeated.

The wind rustled in the newly leafed trees. He heard the neigh of a restless pony, a soft-winged beat that was probably an owl soaring the night. He could hear the beat of hearts, too; his, certainly—probably Sweet Grass Woman's also—maybe even that of the unborn baby. When she stirred, only slightly, he murmured, "Yes, I am happy too."

Like frost, moonlight lay on the hills. Threads of scent twined into his nostrils—rich moist earth, growing things, dung of ponies, dying fires, the cold clean smell of moonlight. Did moonlight smell? Savoring the night, he thought it did. The people slept; free people, living with the earth rather than merely on it. Back east, he thought in fancy, Government clerks would soon be rising from narrow walled-in beds, taking the horse cars to musty offices where they would plot the end of this free Indian life. The moon riding overhead—that Sioux hunter's moon—would appear to those Government people low in the west, setting, falling. That seemed an omen, an evil omen.

There was, of course, only one answer to his dilemma. For months he had lived as a Sioux, grown to like and respect them, have sympathy for their cause. But for all that, he was still one of The People With Hats. Though he had shared Oglala food, their lodges, their friendship, even loved them, many of them—a reserved and diffident man, he winced at the word—he himself was no Sioux. He could not change the color of his skin. He was irrevocably one of The People With Hats. It was heritage in his bone, his flesh, his blood, no less than in all others of his race: his deaf-mute father and mother back in Springfield, old Professor Hinkle at the Academy, Major Cushing at Fort Pike, Bertha Rambouillet and her girls at Fitch's Landing, Andy Wyatt and Clara—even old Cletus Wiley, for all his savage and uncouth ways. Samuel Penrose Blair was not, could not be, could not be expected to be, a Sioux. His destiny lay, had to lie, with The People With Hats.

Sweet Grass Woman was young and attractive, a good cook and a skilled seamstress. The unattached men often cast admiring glances at her. She was chaste, another virtue prized by the Sioux. Soon she would find another husband. Besides, all the children in the Oglala society were mothered and fathered by everyone in the tribe. The child—their unborn child—would never lack for love and affection, even in the absence of the blood father.

Reluctantly convincing himself, he left her sleeping and sat till dawn on a rocky spire overlooking the valley of the Tongue. The Oglalas called it the Torn War Bonnet River, from some ancient happening memorialized in their Winter Calendar that ran back for centuries. When the rising sun splashed blood on the eastern peaks, he rose and went back to the blanket-shrouded shelter. The camp was waking, preparing to move north again.

Sweet Grass Woman cooked his breakfast. So many times she had done so; this summer morning the simple act pierced him like a knife. He would miss her. He would always miss her.

Shadows long on the dew-spangled grass, the Oglalas moved out again. The men of the warrior societies urged their ponies along the line of march, keeping order; joking here, warning there, restraining too-high spirits among the young men, helping the old and sick. Left Hand rode at the head of the great column. Old Bird Talker was at his side to divine the winds, read the movement of clouds, pray for Wakan Tanka's blessing on this sun-drenched morning.

Suddenly making up his mind, Sam muttered an excuse to Sweet Grass Woman, riding in a travois, and clapped moccasined heels to his pony. Trotting to the head of the procession, he respectfully dismounted and signed to Left Hand for permission to speak.

"Father, I—I—" Stammering, he started over. "Father, I have a wish. I prayed to the gods for a long time, and they told me what to do. I—I—"

Bird Talker was pulling at the chief's sleeve. Left Hand took his gaze from Sam and stared at the copse of trees on their flank. Outriders were returning in haste. One flashed a beam of sunlight from a hand mirror to signal danger. Another howled a warning cry, like a wolf.

"*Nutska we hoo!*" Bird Talker muttered. "They say 'white soldiers again!'"

A swift-riding scout pulled up his pony so short the animal sat ludicrously on its haunches, startled.

"White soldiers!" he confirmed, pointing.

On the grassy plain far below, half-hidden among the giant cottonwoods that fringed the river, rode mounted soldiers. At that distance they appeared like tiny toys sprinkled on a green cloth. Then a stray beam of sunlight glanced off something shiny, probably a trooper's bugle. As they watched, there came faintly to their ears the brazen clamor of a trumpet.

Quickly Left Hand snapped orders. The warrior-society men crowded round, dashing away in sequence as each was instructed to some particular duty. Some gathered friends and galloped off in flanking movements. Others were assigned diversionary tactics to keep the soldiers away from vulnerable areas—the rolled lodges and poles, meat, ammunition, especially the women and children, the aged and infirm. Quickly the long and straggling column coalesced. Its track veered into the trees mantling the slopes.

Frustrated, Sam stood holding the hackamore of the pony, dazed by the sudden turn of events. The column they had seen before had obviously changed course and cut across their path. That unexpected action had disrupted the smooth northward progress of the Oglala train. But no less did it disrupt Sam Blair's own plans—perhaps his life.

Though he was not a profane man, he cursed between clenched teeth. "Jesus!"

Fate was being forced on the Oglalas, and on him also. Later, the meeting of the two forces would be called the Battle of the Rosebud after the canyon-deep river that lay between the migrating Sioux and General George Crook's soldiers.

CHAPTER 8

It was in The Moon When Chokecherries Are Ripe that the Oglalas were surprised by the pony soldiers. At that point the Rosebud lay in a grassy amphitheater covered with wild roses and phlox. From the plain rose high walls of sandstone cut by a succession of canyons choked with scrub pine and cedar. On the heights above, the Oglalas reproached themselves for having been thus outflanked. They did not want to fight; they only wanted to hunt. Now there was no choice. The soldiers, spreading across the river, blocked their path.

Galloping to the travois and Sweet Grass Woman, Sam grabbed the hackamore and dragged the horse into the cover of the trees. All round him were shouting and confusion. Old and sick, women and children hurried to cover. Ponies reared and kicked, dogs barked. Children, excited, ran about and called to each other as in a wild game. Men of the warrior societies struggled to maintain order. An old man bowed under the weight of a painted leather chest fell down; Sam picked him up and set him on his feet again. Big Throat, solicitous of Sweet Grass Woman's condition, helped her from the travois and spread a blanket on the ground.

"Here!" Sam handed Big Throat the Starr revolver. "Take care of my woman for me!" Grasping Sweet Grass Woman's hand for a moment, he smiled at her. The dark eyes looked warmly back into his.

"I am not afraid," she assured him.

"You are a brave woman." He nodded. "A good woman!"

Searching in the travois, he came at last on his medical satchel, opening it to make sure all was in order.

"What are you doing?" Big Throat called.

"People are going to be hurt," he said. "They will need help."

Throwing a leg over his pony, he rode out into the sunshine. Dancer dashed by him, ribbons fluttering from his coupstick. Sam called to him but the young man did not hear. Dancer sawed at the nose-rope, and the speckled pony plunged into a rocky defile leading down to the plain. The young man was intent on the important business of counting coup.

From a vantage point at the edge of the sandstone cliffs, Sam could see the battle develop. The Oglalas were outnumbered. The soldiers had brought almost a separate army of mercenary Indian scouts, probably Crows and Shoshones. These took the first shock of the Oglala charge. Ribboned lances flashed in the sun, horses squealed and kicked and fell, a cloud of dust rose from the encounter. To Sam's ear came a faraway popping of guns. Behind the Crows and Shoshones the soldiers advanced in skirmish lines, kneeling and firing. *Hundreds,* he thought. *Hundreds!* This was a major force in the Yellowstone country, part of an extensive and well-prepared campaign against the Sioux.

Clapping heels to his pony, he followed Dancer's headlong path to the canyon. Halfway down, the floor of the defile dropped, a sheer falling-away of ten or twelve feet. Coming on it too suddenly to stop, his mount sailed spraddled-legged into midair. When they hit the sandy bottom the pony rolled sidewise, kicking. Sam was thrown clear. Staggering to his feet, wind knocked out, he watched the frightened pony struggle up and trot rolling-eyed away.

Picking up his satchel, he ran down the canyon. His moccasins slid in the sandy bottom. Burrs and cactus spines, gnarled junipers, caught at his leggings. The battle had already spread. At the mouth of the canyon he saw fighting—a confused moiling of Crow and Sioux in sun-shot clouds of dust. The report of guns, echoing from the canyon walls, deafened him.

"Mini!" someone called. *"Mini!"*

It was the Sioux word for *water.* Propped against the canyon wall was Smoke Eater, the young man who always won most of the Oglala horse races. Smoke Eater had been shot in the face. His nose was smashed askew, and he was blinded.

"Mini!" he repeated. *"Aaiiee—mini!"*

Sam knelt beside him. He had no water but in his bag was a small flask of whisky.

"Who?" Smoke Eater asked. "Who?"

"I am Lightning Man," Sam explained. He gave Smoke Eater an

opium pill. "Drink this!" Upending the flask, he poured whisky into the pain-twisted mouth. It was all he could do.

"Lightning Man?"

"Yes."

Smoke Eater nodded, lay back.

"I can't see! How can a man fight when he can't see?" One hand searched for the carbine lying in the dirt. "I want my gun! Lightning Man, give me my gun!"

Sam put it in the groping hand.

"You will be all right," he assured the youth. "I know it!"

Smoke Eater's head bobbed in thanks. "Hie, hie." The single eagle feather drooped sideways. As Sam picked up his bag again, Smoke Eater was trying to prop his feather upright.

Staying close to the walls, Sam worked his way along the cliffs, wincing at the noise, shrinking as random shots spanged against the sandstone over his head and sent down showers of reddish dust. A riderless horse with a McClellan saddle skittered sidewise past him, nostrils flared. In the dense underbrush he could no longer observe the progress of the battle and wandered about, clutching his satchel. Suddenly, before him, a tangle of bushes swayed, splintered. A nearly naked Oglala and his opponent—a Crow, Sam supposed—broke through the wiry screen and fell locked in combat. The Crow screamed out an imprecation and swung his hatchet but the Oglala, a young man whom Sam recognized, slid his knife into the belly and ripped upward.

The Crow's face wrinkled in surprise. Dropping the hatchet, he slid down, clutching at his slayer's legs. Finally his grip relaxed. He lay still, breathing heavily, in a tangle of pinkish intestine. Sliding the bloody knife into his belt, the Oglala searched the junipers for his rifle. Finding it, he straightened, seeing Sam Blair for the first time.

"*Hoka hey!*" he grinned, brandishing the gun. "Lightning Man, it is a good day to fight!" Eagerly he raced toward the main engagement, singing his war song as he ran:

> "*I am going to look for the enemy.*
> *When I find him I will kill him*
> *Or he will kill me! I do not know!*
> *But only the rocks live forever.*"

Already the unfortunate Crow was stiffening in death. Not knowing why, except he felt he had to do something—the Crow had been a brave man—Sam dragged the body up a gravelly rise and laid it beside a pool of muddy water bordered with reeds. From that point he could watch more of the fighting. It was apparent the Oglalas were hard-pressed. The soldiers and their Crow allies, pushed the Oglalas against the base of the cliffs where there was little room for ponies to maneuver. Sam's own position was dangerous. Shooting too high, as the Sioux claimed The People With Hats always did, the soldiers' leaden slugs whistled over his head, sent puffs of dust from the cliffs, whanged and whined as they ricocheted up the canyon. Echoes of their flight sounded like banshees. Almost at Sam's feet a band of flannel-shirted cavalrymen broke through the Sioux lines and flung itself like a wave up the canyon. Turning, the horsemen galloped back into the fray, a young trumpeter, bugle to his lips, sounding a wild paean.

Sam shrank back. In Sioux shirt and moccasins he was enemy to the galloping troopers. But as the file clattered by, the bugler toppled from the saddle and fell heavily. The shiny trumpet bounced from one ledge of rock to another.

The young man tried to get to his feet. Propping a hand against the ground, he suddenly collapsed in pain. Running to him, Sam saw a vagrant ball had broken the soldier's arm; radius and ulna were splintered. As Sam loomed over him the trooper tried to roll away, making an ineffectual try at shielding his face from the hatchet he knew would quickly descend.

"Don't be afraid," Sam blurted. "I'm a—a—" For a dreadful moment he paused. *What, exactly, was he?* "I—I'm a doctor," he decided. "Here—let me look at your arm!"

The boy continued to stare, forgetting the pain of his wounds. He drew sharply away when Sam tried to separate the bloody sleeve from splintered bones.

"You're a Goddamned Sioux!"

Sam opened his satchel. "I'm white as you are!"

"Then what in hell are you doing here? Dressed up in those—those clothes?" The trooper bit his lip in agony.

"No time to explain now," Sam said.

He gave the boy whisky laced with tincture of opium, and

twisted off willow branches for splints. "What's your name?" he asked, tearing strips from the trooper's flannel shirt.

"Kelly," the trooper gasped, biting his lip as he watched Sam wrap strips round the shattered arm.

"Eh?"

"Name's John Kelly, Third Cavalry! B Company!"

A fusillade, nearer now, clipped branches from the low-spreading junipers in which Sam worked. He blinked, wiped eyes stung by rock fragments. A handful of Oglalas—Sam recognized Tall Horse and Big Tree Man and Dancer—ran past him to scramble up the steep slope, gun in one hand and the other clutching bushes and stunted pines to aid in the ascent. Apparently they were preparing to ambush the soldiers if the Oglalas were driven into the narrow canyon.

"Here!" Sam offered, handing the boy his trumpet.

Kelly made an ineffectual motion with his free hand.

"I'll just put it in your lap," Sam offered.

It was apparent he had better to leave the canyon and climb back to the heights as soon as possible. Already, above the scattered brush, he saw a red and white cavalry pennon bobbing about on a staff. The soldiers were very near. The Sioux garb made him a likely target.

"Kelly?" Sam asked.

The young man opened eyes already made dull by the heavy dose of opium and whisky. "Yeah—Doc, or whatever in hell you are!"

"What day is this?"

"Saturday, I think. Or maybe Friday. I dunno."

"I mean—what date?" Sam had long been without any knowledge of white man's time.

"The date?"

Something tore at Sam's beaded shirt. There was a ripping sound. He looked down at a dangling bit of fringe. That bullet had been close!

"I ain't likely to forget!" the bugler murmured. Almost drunkenly, his head rolled. "The seventeenth of June," he said, tongue thick. "My—my birthday was yesterday." Head falling sidewise, he rolled down in the bushes almost comfortably, overtaken by sleep.

The Battle of the Rosebud would have been a disaster for Left Hand and his wandering Oglalas if Cheyenne friends had not arrived to help. Scouts from the Fat Grass encampment had for days watched Crook's forces. Expecting an attack on the gathering of Sioux and Cheyennes, a picked band of Cheyenne warriors moved down the Rosebud, interposing themselves between Crook's forces and the teeming Indian encampment on the Fat Grass River.

Arriving as the desperate Oglalas were driven up the canyon, the Cheyennes flanked the soldiers on the plain and rolled them back. Outnumbered and outfought, the soldiers retreated. Now they were scurrying down Goose Creek toward their base at the foot of the Big Horn mountains, along with wagons and beef herds. One arm of the three-pronged drive Cletus Wiley spoke of was effectually crippled. Lightning Man had again brought the Oglalas good luck.

Dancer was in a good mood. He had counted coup twice with his long beribboned wand. Now it was decorated with a sandy-haired scalp. As Sam looked at it, proudly shown, he swallowed hard, felt queasy. This was a white man's scalp; the hair of one of his own

"Those Cheyenne brothers!" Dancer marveled. "They had *girl* kind—it could belong to Luther Speck!
horseholders! I never saw anything like that! Imagine! Girls!"

They sat at a small fire, enjoying buffalo ribs with scarce salt bartered from the Cheyennes. During the winter the Oglalas ran short of salt, ordinarily obtained during the summer from beds near the Powder River. They had had to make do with gall from the livers of buffalo. Gall was an acceptable substitute, but real salt was a treat.

"The Cheyennes are good fighters," Dancer went on. "But I do not think we really needed them! We would have won anyway!"

It was a young warrior's enthusiasm. Sam said nothing. There were still the other two prongs of The People With Hats: Terry and Custer.

"Here!" Affable, Dancer handed him a thick tablet. "When the soldiers ran away I picked this up. It is for you."

On the first page were some scribbled words; *Dear Phoebe; write you these few lines before we*—The letters straggled off in a jagged scrawl as if the writer had been interrupted.

"Hie," Sam said. "Hie, hie."

"I thought," Dancer remarked, arranging his coiffure with his scratching stick, "I would keep it and write on paper the way you showed me, friend. But I changed my mind."

Sweet Grass Woman and Chickadee slept soundly in the blanketed shelter, gathering strength for the trip on the morrow to the Fat Grass camp. Sam tore off the scribbled page and folded it carefully. He did not know what to do with it.

"Changed your mind? Why?"

Dancer's eyes sparkled with good-humored malice.

"I think I do not need to learn English, friend! You see what we did to The People With Hats today? Soon we are going to beat them all. We will drive them back to where the sun comes up. We will push them into the water. They will have to swim to the other side. Then all the land—" He swept out his arms; firelight glowed on the glistening taut skin, winked on prized copper and brass armlets. "All the land will be ours again! There will not be any white men!" He grinned. "No one will need to speak English! Everyone speaks Sioux! That is all there is to it!"

Sam's face was troubled. Dancer, contrite, touched his hand. "Friend, I am only having fun with you!"

Sam scratched in the dirt with a rib bone. "My heart is laid on the ground," he admitted.

"I know that." Dancer examined his carved and painted scratching stick. "You are two men! I understand."

"No," Sam corrected. "I am *one* man! I am one of The People With Hats. I can never be anything else." Almost without thinking, the Sioux words came quickly, easily. His hands moved in the firelight, flowing from one gesture to the other. "Soon I must go back to them. I love my Sioux brothers. But I must go back!"

Dancer's eyes narrowed. "Go back?" He shook his head. "Go back? Now you are telling me a joke!"

Sam shook his head. "It is not a joke."

Dancer frowned. "Do not talk that way! It is dangerous!"

"You are our good luck!" Agitated, Dancer rose to stalk about the lodge. "Do you think Left Hand and Bird Talker can let you go back now to The People With Hats?"

"But I—"

"The Oglalas need you! You are our big medicine! The people

cannot let you go away now, friend!" Concerned, Dancer pulled at his lip, stared at Sam. "Let me tell you—if you try to go away, they will send the Bad Faces after you!"

Sam was offended by Dancer's threats. "Listen!" he said. "Listen to me!" But Dancer interrupted again.

"Anyway, your woman is going to have a baby. I don't think you ought to go and leave her that way! That is the way bad white men have always done with our women! And you are not bad, Lightning Man. You are good. You belong with us, not with those People With Hats! You are an Oglala brother—brother to me, to Bird Talker, to Left Hand, to us all!"

Angry, frustrated, repentant—emotion filled Sam's brain. "I do not know what to do!" he shouted. "And, friend, you are not helping me!"

Dancer studied him for a long moment. Then he raised his hand in a quick gesture. *Finished. I have said all I am going to say.* Turning on his heel, he left Sam's lodge and strode toward the grassy meadow where the Oglalas and their Cheyenne friends were celebrating the big fight, recounting coups and telling stories of their experiences during the battle. With sinking heart Sam watched Dancer's retreating figure until it was lost in the dancing shadows around the big fire. *He has gone,* he thought, *to tell the Bad Faces to keep an eye on me.*

Perhaps he could have fled—he did not like the word, but it was an apt description—he could have fled during the Rosebud fight. But then, he had felt obliged as a physician to treat the wounded, red or white. Too, his Indian garb made it dangerous to attempt on short notice to go over to the other side. If he were really going to try it, there would have to be preparations made—proper clothing, food, a weapon. But it would be hard now to leave the camp on any pretext. He would be watched.

Standing at the doorflap, he listened to the sounds of revelry. At a late hour he finally lay down with Sweet Grass Woman. She stirred, then was quiet, breast rising and falling in regular rhythm. Sam could not sleep. Once he thought he dozed, but twitched at an imagined step nearby. Were the Bad Faces watching him already?

The next morning, Three Star Crook's invading force safely out of the way at the foot of the Big Horns, the Oglalas resumed the journey. Lying in the travois, Sweet Grass Woman was quiet. When the long train stopped for a noontime meal, she ate only a corncake and drank a sip of tea. Big Throat urged her to eat more.

"You have got to remember the child inside you is hungry even if you are not!"

Sam, too, wanted her to eat. She shook her head.

"I cannot eat anymore. It sticks in my throat."

That night, only a few miles short of the big encampment, Left Hand's band and their Cheyenne escorts stopped in a grassy glade along the river. The night was still and moonless, a velvety black riddled with stars. Sweet Grass Woman was again without appetite. Sam, ridden by doubts and fears, became annoyed.

"You must eat!" he blurted, holding out a section of crisp brown buffalo gut he had spiraled onto a green twig and toasted before the fire. It was a delicacy Sweet Grass Woman was fond of. This time she only looked away, pulling the blanket around her shoulders.

"Are you sick?"

"Perhaps."

He knew the nausea common to pregnant females. This was only sulkiness. Impatiently he demanded, "Are you angry?"

She turned a stricken face. "No."

"Then what is the matter?"

She hid her face in the blanket. Ashamed of his conduct, yet feeling himself badly used, he ate the roasted gut himself. After a while he made a small shelter for her to sleep in. When he returned to the dying fire she was gone. Anxious, he walked among the chatting women.

"I have not seen her," they said, and went on with the latest camp gossip.

Big Throat joined him in the search. At last Sam found her, muffled in her blanket, sitting on a ledge at the periphery of the light from the campfires.

"It is getting cold," he warned. "You should go to bed and keep warm!"

She did not answer.

In spite of annoyance he managed to keep his voice gentle. "What is wrong?"

Suddenly she rose, flung arms about him. The blanket fell unheeded to the ground.

"I am sad! My life is not worth living!"

He felt his heart melt. "But—but why? What is wrong?"

She lay her head against his shoulder and he smelled the fragrance of her hair. In the starlight he saw the pale line of the part in the black locks.

"You do not love me any more! I—I have done something bad, and you do not love me!"

He kissed the parting. "No! That is foolish!"

"But I know you do not love me! You do not talk to me any more. You do not make jokes. When we sleep, you stay away and do not touch me. You lie awake and think bad things." She thrust out her thumb in the Sioux gesture. *I speak truth.* "There is no way a man can fool a woman about a thing like that!"

Contrite, he pressed her to him. "No! That is not true! It is only that I—that I—"

How to explain to her the trouble, the black dog that lay on his back? That would only make it worse.

"It is not true," he said lamely. "I love you very much!"

She was silent and he, embarrassed and frustrated. Awkwardly he stroked her hair.

"It is just that—"

Again he did not know what to say. Torn and uncertain, he pulled her down into the grass beside him. For a long time they lay, heads pillowed on the folded blanket, staring at the stars. Each, he supposed, had private thoughts. He knew his, but was not sure of those of Sweet Grass Woman. Disregarding the blanketed shelter, they slept together, waking in dew-diamonded grass to complete the journey to the Fat Grass conclave.

Next morning Sam caught his breath at the size of the camp, the extent of a good-sized Illinois city. Along the river stretched a forest of lodges. Each group had its own area—the Hunkpapas, Miniconjous, Blackfeet, Sans Arcs, Brulés, Cheyennes, and now Left Hand and his Oglalas. At this point the Little Big Horn, fringed with cottonwoods, made a sweeping S-shaped curve. North of the curve lay the Indian camp, with plenty of water, game, and lush grass made rich by droppings of thousands of generations of buffalo. To the east was a high ridge covered with Spanish dagger and sagebrush, over which the sun rose as Left Hand's band rode into camp. They were greeted by barking dogs, excited children, women cooking breakfast at hundreds of small fires.

Dancer, kneeing his pony beside Sam, was enthusiastic. "Did you ever see so many people!" he marveled. "There can never be so many People With Hats! And they could never own so many horses! Look!"

In makeshift corrals, edged with piles of sagebrush, were thousands of ponies, peacefully cropping the long grass. As a conservative estimate Sam reckoned about fifteen or twenty horses and three warriors to a lodge. He tried to calculate the number of tipis and gave up. There were thousands of warriors on the Little Big Horn, tens of thousands of ponies.

With Dancer's help he erected their own lodge in the Oglala circle. The Cheyennes, claimants to being the oldest foes of The People With Hats, camped to the north, the post of honor. Any attack by the white soldiers would come from that direction, along the backside of the ridge for concealment, then breaking out and sweeping down on the camp across a shallow ford in the river. Sam and Big Throat made a comfortable bed for Sweet Grass Woman, who was near her time.

"I am going to walk around the camp," he told Sweet Grass Woman.

"I will go with you," Dancer offered. "I have a lot of friends to talk to."

Along the ridge, children played a game with smoking brands snatched from cooking fires. Each side piled up great mounds of dry brush. The object of the game seemed to be to set the opponents' brushpile on fire with brands thrown from a line scratched in the dirt. Old men sat in the morning sun making arrows, straightening the shaft by drawing it repeatedly through the hole in a deer vertebra. Young girls dug for roots and Indian turnips, gathered greens and herbs. The women cooked in outdoor shelters while the husbands and young bachelors sat at the doorways of lodges, painting themselves, arranging coiffures, and primping. Low over the camp lay a pall of fragrant gray woodsmoke. The air was filled with singing, laughing, the barking of camp dogs and the neighs of frisky war ponies, kicking up heels and prancing in the brush corrals.

Dancer carried his coupstick proudly and ostentatiously. Somehow he managed to call attention to it wherever they stopped. To a Sans Arc friend admiring his image in a small mirror, Dancer remarked, "Two days ago I slapped a pony-soldier across the face with this very stick! He tried to pull it away from me but I hit him with my hatchet and he fell down." To a Brulé hammering out arrow points, Dancer objected. "I do not like metal points! I always use the good flint ones made by our old Oglala men!" He fingered the sandy-haired scalp. "I shot this white man with one of my flint-point arrows. He dropped like a buffalo and did not move even when I pulled off his hair!"

During the next several days there was continual oratory. Gathering in a grassy vale along the river the people listened to speakers —brave and honored men like Crazy Horse and Sitting Bull, Gall and Black Elk. Though most of the chiefs were older men, Sitting Bull appeared only in his late twenties. Relatively short—no more than five feet eight inches—he was strong and sinewy, arms heavily scarred from a recent Sun Dance ceremony. His manner, even when making an important statement, remained reflective and melancholy, though the usual Indian speech-making style was fevered and impassioned.

"He is a great man," Dancer whispered in Sam's ear.

It was odd; Dancer seemed to be always with Sam Blair. Had Dancer himself been told to watch him? Or was Sam, under the weight of his dilemma, becoming unbalanced?

Waking early, after a bad dream, he squatted in the doorway watching Sweet Grass Woman cook his breakfast: prickly-pear cactus fruits, sliced thin and fried in hump fat. Too, there were the peeled, sweet thistle stalks tasting almost like bananas, the rare tropical fruit that seldom came to Springfield when he was a boy. In spite of his protests Sweet Grass Woman, heavy with child, insisted on rising early to collect and prepare the thistle stalks, knowing he liked then. The loving action unsettled him; this morning he had been trying to prepare himself to leave her, to strike out for old Fort Tullock where the Big Horn entered the Yellowstone.

He would be safe there, for a while, until he decided on California or Oregon.

Sitting near him, hands in lap, her legs were modestly folded to one side. It was considered indelicate for an Indian woman to squat as men did.

"Do you like the food?" she asked.

He nodded, not trusting words.

"You—you are thinking—what?" She made the sign: fingers extended, pointing to different directions. *What?*

Dismally he chewed on the flesh of the cactus fruit. It tasted like wood in his mouth. "I—I—" Stammering, he could not find the words and fell silent. Outside there were early morning sounds. A crier rode among the lodges, calling out the news. Children screamed in excitement, a pony neighed. *It has to be this way,* he thought. *There is no other way. It is a kindness to her to go.*

"I love you," Sweet Grass Woman murmured, eyes downcast. "You are all I ever loved."

The words tore his heart. Hearing them, understanding, he nevertheless turned his face blindly toward her. "What? What did you say?"

The voice of the crier became louder, excited. More ponies neighed. There was a thudding of hoofs; someone blew an eagle-bone whistle. He spat out the remnants of the cactus fruit, listened. Sweet Grass Woman did not seem to notice. She remained in a submissive position, head bowed and hands in her lap. *Waiting. Waiting.*

As in a daze the import of the crier's voice sank into Sam's consciousness. "Drive all the horse herds into the camp circle! Women, be ready to move quickly but stay calm! You will all be protected! Men, prepare yourselves to fight!"

Jumping to his feet, he held aside the tent flap. The camp moiled and bubbled in activity. Women ran about, gathering up children. Horses reared and pranced while men tugged at hackamores. Struggling, a pony kicked out and knocked over a cooking shelter. The dry leaves thatching it caught fire, a stewpot overturned. An old man carrying a sheaf of newly made arrows hobbled past, assisted by his wife.

"What is it?" Sweet Grass Woman asked, her voice fearful.

He did not need to reply. Running up came Dancer, coupstick in one hand and repeating rifle in the other.

"There you are, Lightning Man!"

"I am here," Sam admitted. "But what is happening?"

The young man pointed excitedly toward the lower end of the camp, below the great S-shaped bend.

"It is Pa Huska!" he cried. "Long Hair, with his white soldiers! Oh, a lot of soldiers! Red Horse and some women were up the river digging turnips and saw them. This time we have got them all in one place! We can kill them all!" He whooped with joy. "Today is a fine day to fight!" Waving his coupstick high, Dancer dashed toward the bend of the river.

CHAPTER 9

Sam ran into the lodge. In the confusion of battle was a good time to leave the village. He could hide in the hills, look for a chance to join the invading troops of the man the Oglalas called Pa Huska—Long Hair. Of course, the soldiers would not know him from a Sioux and would probably shoot at him. That was a chance he had to take. But he would need certain things. Rummaging in the litter at the rear of the lodge, he found his medical satchel and snatched it up. The Magnetic Tractors lay in the gloom, metal electrodes dully shining. He would have to abandon them. Some day he must pay Dr. Perkins, their inventor.

"Where is my gun?" he asked. He had not seen the Starr revolver for some time.

Following him about, Sweet Grass Woman watched him, dark eyes filled with surmise.

"The revolver!" he insisted. "My Starr revolver!" Surely she could not misunderstand. He made the sign, indicating the rotation of the cylinder. "Where is it?"

She avoided his eye.

"Where is it?" he insisted, and caught her by the wrist.

She still did not look at him but spoke in a low voice. "The Bad Faces took it."

"The Bad Faces?" He was perplexed. "But why?"

"I—I did not want them to! But they came while you were gone and took it."

Had Dancer gone to the Bad Faces and told them his suspicions? Was that the reason the Bad Faces had taken away his gun, fearing a traitorous action on his part? He could hardly believe it; the whole thing seemed unreal, like a dream. Still—Dancer had stayed close to him all this time, as if watching.

"Why didn't you tell me?" he asked Sweet Grass Woman. Awk-wardly she tried to put her cheek against his. He pushed her away. Chickadee, conscious of tension, watched them with wide eyes, spoon poised halfway to mouth.

"Why didn't you tell me?" Sam insisted.

"Dancer said no. The Bad Faces said no. I was forbidden to tell you."

"But why—"

"They were afraid," she explained. "They were afraid you were going to go away, take away the people's luck, and maybe tell all about us to Pa Huska." She fell silent, though he suspected she wanted to say more—say that she, too, feared he would go away. He had not been successful in keeping his plans secret.

"Are you angry?" Her voice was meek.

Through the thin-scraped skins, radiant with mellow sunlight, he could hear guns, war whoops, neighs of frightened horses—the an-cient clamor of battle.

"No, I am not angry," he said, "but you had better take the boy and go with the other women up on the hills where the soldiers cannot hurt you." Already he heard the commands of the camp police, herding women and children to safety.

"No!" she protested.

"But you must!"

She clung to him. "You stay, I stay! There is no place I want to be without you!"

Frustrated, he went to the doorway and looked out. At the bend of the river all was confusion; there was a great cloud of dust. To see better, Sam climbed the spindly wooden meat rack at the door of the lodge.

In the scrub-willow and buffalo-berry bushes men were fighting. High above the dust waved a cavalry guidon. From its movement Sam judged the soldiers had been thrown back already by the horde of Sioux warriors. The cavalry, unsuccessful in the precipi-tate attack, was pushed across a shallow ford in the Fat Grass River. A few soldiers were apparently cut off in the brush, because the Sioux had set fire to dry buffalo grass and sage to drive them out.

Now he could see soldiers retreating beyond the river. Many

were mounted and galloping up the hill. Others had lost their mounts in the battle and scrambled and dodged up the slope as best they could. Some fell as the Sioux, firing upward, caught them in frantic flight. Riderless horses ran back and forth across the cactus-studded hillside, reins dangling. Sam could hear the Sioux warriors yipping in triumph like coyotes.

On the hillside soldiers were trying to reform their ranks. The mounted men got down and started to dig entrenchments. Others took the horses in groups of four and lead them into the shelter of a grove of trees. The cavalrymen had been badly mauled, and the threat from that direction was over. The Sioux, leaving a few men to harass the soldiers on the hill, came crashing back through the camp in a great rush of men and ponies, waving weapons in triumph, shouting. Sam watched as the cavalcade swept by, pony tails tied up for war. Now the Sioux forces were galloping toward the northern end of the camp, at the end of the long ridge. In the boiling dust stirred by the hoofs of the ponies he saw Dancer, exultant, one hand holding the reins and the other waving his coupstick high. *Three coups,* Dancer had said, *and then I die.*

Sam listened to the far-off popping of guns from the Cheyenne village to the north. Vision cut off by the long ridge, he could see nothing.

The seventeenth, that had been the fight on the Rosebud. Today, then, was—what? The twenty-fifth. That would make it a Sunday. The Sabbath, the Lord's Day. His lips twisted at the irony.

Unknown to him, Sweet Grass Woman had been standing in the doorway of the lodge. "Look!" she called, pointing. At the base of the ridge was a group of riders, too distant to be made out. Sioux— or Pa Huska's men?

Riders streamed endlessly around the base of the ridge. They could hear shrill cries of victory, see water splashing in the sun as the Sioux ponies galloped across the ford on their way back to camp.

"They are our people!" she said, exultant.

Sam looked again at the sun. It was overhead. In less than two hours the Sioux had defeated Pa Huska and his troops. There were still, of course, a few soldiers on the hill up the river. But they were bottled up, and would probably be picked off at leisure.

Slowly he climbed down from the meat rack, watching the Sioux return in shrill-lunged victory. He felt as tired and defeated as the cavalrymen.

That night there was a celebration, a victory dance along the river. Bonfires burned. Men and women and children joined in a shuffling procession around the fire, chanting thanks to Wakan Tanka, who had delivered Pa Huska and his men into their hands. All night the dancing and the singing went on. Up the river, the fires the Sioux started to drive the fleeing soldiers from the reeds burned also. It seemed there were fires, fires, fires, everywhere; the night was fragrant with smoke.

Dancer, triumphant, visited Sam's lodge waving his coupstick, adorned with a new scalp. "It was very strange," he reported. "This soldier was hiding in the grass! I saw him and hit him in the face with my coupstick. He threw down his rifle and ran like a rabbit. I went after him, and just as I was going to catch him he turned around and screamed. Then he pulled the revolver out of his holster and put it to his own head." Enjoying the story, he paused for effect, looking from Sam to Sweet Grass Woman to Chickadee. The child's eyes glistened with excitement. "Can you imagine!" Dancer marveled. "That soldier blew out his brains, his *own* brains!"

Sam's mouth was dry. A pulse sounded in his ears as he looked at the scalp. *How much does it take to convince me that these are savages, barbarous savages—not human beings?*

"What—what happened down the river, at the end of the ridge?"

Dancer fondled the fresh scalp. "When we drove those few soldiers up on the hill we heard Pa Huska and his men were riding along in back of that ridge, planning to surprise us, just the way we thought. So we all hurried back through our camp and down to the ford. When we got there we saw Pa Huska and his men coming toward us. We met them there, on the hill above the ford, and killed them, every one!"

Chickadee clapped his hands. Sweet Grass Woman glanced uncertainly at Sam.

"Every one?" Sam asked, unbelieving.

Dancer nodded vigorously. "Not one was left!"

Sam swallowed hard. A company? Two companies? "How many?"

Dancer flung out fingers in tens, the Indian way of counting. Sam watched. *Fifty, a hundred—*He could not believe it. *A hundred and fifty, two hundred—*Dancer ended with a few fingers. *Two hundred odd!* "And all dead?"

"We killed everybody!" Dancer exulted. He picked up Chickadee, holding the child high in the firelight. "You should have been there, boy!" he chuckled. "There will never be another fight like that! Our grandchildren will still be talking about it! Forever we have driven The People With Hats out of our land!"

"Pa Huska, too?" Sam asked in disbelief. "You killed Pa Huska?"

"Pa Huska," Dancer boasted, "and all of his men!"

"Those soldiers that were on the hill. Are they still there?"

Dancer shrugged. "We do not care about them. There are only a few. Sitting Bull told some of the Bad Faces to stay there and keep shooting at them. I think he wanted to leave a few alive so they could go back and tell The People With Hats never to come into Sioux lands again."

Some soldiers were still alive, on the hill!

"Well," Dancer concluded, "I want to go now and join the dancing. I have got to thank Wakan Tanka for giving me my coups." Proudly carrying the coupstick, he left the lodge. Sam remained squatting by the fire.

"Are you hungry?" Sweet Grass Woman asked.

His mind in ferment, he shook his head.

"It is time to eat," she urged. "I will fix whatever you want."

"Feed the boy! I am not hungry."

While she was busy preparing food for Chickadee, he opened the flap and looked out at the celebration. Dancers milled in concentric circles, great black snakes writhing in coils to the beat of drums. Smoke drifted through the throng. Fires burned everywhere.

This was a great event for the Sioux nation, one that no man would want to miss. For the moment Sam appeared to be free. He looked up the river, toward the hillside where the beleaguered remnant of Custer's force was dug in. There would be wounded up there, men who needed help, he told himself.

The hour was late. Sweet Grass Woman and Chickadee already slept, the boy cuddled against the swollen stomach, her arm protectively across the baby-fat body. In the dying firelight Sam looked down on her. Against his will, his eyes filled with tears. He almost spoke her name. He loved her. He loved Sweet Grass Woman in a way he had never loved Clara Freeman, yet he was leaving her.

Soundlessly his lips moved, forming her name.

"Sha, sha," he whispered. "Ah, you are beautiful!"

He had never been much on art, but remembered a picture he had seen in a book; a painting by Bottle somebody—an Italian name. *Mother and child.* He felt muscles in his throat tighten. *Oglala mother and child. His child, in her belly.* Now he was going to betray her. But there was no other way! After all, he was merely a creature of circumstance. He had not asked for these things to happen! If cases had not gone awry, if the rains had not come, if the crops had been good, he might even now be living with Clara at Fitch's Landing, settled down, with a good practice, raising children—white children—with golden hair like Clara's, and blue eyes. Sam Blair could hardly be held responsible for the fate of everyone!

Picking up his physician's satchel, he hesitated for a moment, looking at the bulky journal he had kept for so long. He regretted leaving it—all his study of Indian herbs, his hoped for pharmacopoeia, was in those pages—but he could hardly carry it with him. Silently he stepped into the night.

No one seemed to notice. Everyone was dancing, singing, praying to the gods—Rock, Thunder, Buffalo, the Sioux pantheon, the gods who had brought victory to a favored people. Passing between the deserted lodges, he left the Oglala circle and plunged into head-high growth along the river. Here and there brush smoldered, and he had to pick his way under a waning moon. Soon he was smudged and blackened by the burned canes, and tasted soot in his mouth. His moccasins were wet and muddy and the reeds tore at his shirt, sometimes drawing blood. But he bore steadily on, keeping his eye on the hillside where the remaining soldiers were pinned down.

The Bad Faces, Dancer said, were still around, keeping a watch on the besieged soldiers. From time to time Sam paused, standing on a grassy hummock, peering warily. Perhaps even the Bad Faces could not resist the opportunity to join the dancing throng in the meadow.

Suddenly, from the bank of the river, only a hundred yards ahead, a fusillade of shots broke out. He shrank into the reeds, hearing bullets snip the long grasses over his head. A Sioux voice called out a challenge. Then Sam heard a white man's voice, cursing steadily. There was a strange clanking noise, and the reeds were lit with flashes of gunfire. "It's Lieutenant Smith!" someone called. "He's hit bad! Come over here and help me!"

The men on the hill, desperate for water, had probably sent down a party with canteens; that was the reason for the tinny noises. But they had been discovered by the waiting Bad Faces, and the leader was wounded.

Kneeling in the high grasses, Sam listened to the progress of the encounter. Troopers cursed, the lurking Sioux howled and yipped. A man cried out, a scream of pain, and the sound was quickly broken off. There was a satisfied grunt, very near Sam. A voice shouted, "*Onhey! Onhey!*" It was the Sioux cry of victory.

How long he stayed in the reeds he did not know. Finally all was silent; the Sioux had apparently overwhelmed the water party. He poked his head up, parted the reeds. In the pale moonlight he could see little. Down the river there was a red glow in the sky. Faintly, borne on the night wind, came the great chorus of Sioux voices, raised in victory. They were still dancing, celebrating.

Afraid to move, fearing the Bad Faces still lurked in the reeds, he waited. The night wore on. Cold and wet, he shivered. Looking up the hillside, he saw an occasional wink of light, heard a murmur of voices. The soldiers were wondering what had happened to the water detail.

After a long time he parted the reeds again and moved cautiously toward the ford. The Fat Grass was shallow here, only shoulder deep on horses, but moved swiftly. He slid down a muddy bank, sucking in his breath as snow-fed water closed around thighs, chest, swirled about his shoulders, trying to tear the satchel from his grasp. Panicky, his feet sought the bottom. He struggled to hold the precious satchel above his head.

The current swept him downstream toward the Indian camp. He was borne along, bobbing like a cork, trying to sound bottom with

his feet. Then a sudden eddy swept him into a backwater of float-
ing twigs and branches. They caught and tore at him. He held up a
hand to protect his face, but the movement promptly dropped him
to the bottom. He was drowning, he knew it, and flailed in panic.
Suddenly his feet dragged on firm sand. He pushed down, hard,
and managed to propel himself toward a snag around which boiled
white water.

Gasping, he clung to the branch. The shore was near, very near.
He groped his way along the limb, at last finding shallow water.
Out of breath, he crawled through the ooze, then staggered through
still-burning brush to safety.

Sprawling on the bank, he found he still had his precious satchel.
He was covered with greasy soot, plastered with viscous mud. He
he lost a moccasin and tasted blood in a corner of his mouth. Then
he discovered a jagged cut on his forehead, probably where a
branch had poked. He spat out blood and sat for a while, breathing
hard, feeling his heart thud as it pumped to match the tremendous
physical exertion.

What time was it? He looked into the velvety June sky. Orion
was low on the western horizon; it must be near dawn. He got
groggily to his feet and started up the steep slope. The grove of
trees was a darker spot in the starlight. The moon had set.

He picked his way among boulders littering the S-shaped bend of
the river. They had been borne there, he supposed, by floods,
carried down the Fat Grass from the mountains and deposited on
the outside curve of the bank. He climbed over huge stones, sought
his way around others, found lungs again laboring as he climbed.
Turning, he looked to the east. Was that a faint flush, the coming of
dawn? Down the river the red glow still lit the sky.

A vagrant wind rose, bearing to his ears sounds from the soldiers
above. A man called out, a horse neighed. He saw a spark of light;
probably a weary trooper lighting a pipe.

"Hey, up there!" he called. "It's me—Sam Blair!"

The distance was too great. No one heard him. But from below,
across the river, something flashed. A moment later a bullet
spanged into the tumbled rocks, and he heard the report of a rifle.
A Sioux voice yelled. There was an answering scatter of shots from

the trees overhead. He was caught on the hillside between two foes, and dawn was coming. He would have to move somewhere.

Lying back in the rocks, winded, he fought to catch his breath. Below him, against the boulders, moved a faint shadow. He squinted. Was it his fevered imagination? Then he heard a scraping sound. A rock, dislodged, fell away and bounced down the slope.

"Who's there?" he called, voice husky.

No one answered.

He called again; no response. But the shadow flitted across a bone-white slab of rock, and he knew he was followed. Unsteady on his feet he rose. "Who's there?"

A voice answered, and he stiffened in alarm.

"Lightning Man?"

He knew that voice; it was Dancer.

"Lightning Man?" the voice insisted.

He looked round, sought cover. Dancer was coming after him. Not the Bad Faces, but Dancer. He remembered the young man's impassioned words; *You are our good luck! Do you think Left Hand and Bird Talker can let you go back to The People With Hats? You are our big medicine! The people cannot let you go away now, friend!* Dancer had said something else, too. *Anyway, your woman is going to have a baby! I don't think you ought to go and leave her that way.*

"I see you," Dancer called. "You are there, in the rocks!"

He stood motionless, watching Dancer approach. The young man still carried the long coupstick. He appeared to have no weapon but the knife at his belt, and he dripped water. Dancer had swum the river in pursuit of Lightning Man.

"She said you ran away," Dancer told him.

"I am going back to my own people," Sam protested. "It is what I have to do!"

In the darkness he could not see Dancer's face but the voice was determined.

"No," Dancer said, flatly. "That cannot be!"

Sam dropped the satchel. He looked around for something to defend himself. "You cannot stop me!"

Dancer shook his head. "You are a coward! A man who runs away is a coward!" He shook the coupstick. "I did not run away! I

counted coup three times! With my coupstick I struck the men I
killed! They were soldiers. But Lightning Man, you are my friend.
You are a friend of all the Oglalas. I do not want to strike you with
my coupstick! So come back with me! Come back to the people,
come back to the village!"

"No!" Sam blurted.

"It is not too late," Dancer pleaded. He glanced upward, toward
the besieged soldiers. "You do not belong up there. You belong
with us. You are our luck, our medicine!" He took a step toward
Sam, holding out a hand. "Come!"

Sam backed away. "Stand back! I—I'll crack your head with a
rock if you come any closer!"

Dancer paused, hand outstretched.

"You will not come?"

"No. I—I can't!"

Dancer raised the coupstick. It whistled through the air, catching
Sam a stinging blow where neck joined shoulder. The shock seemed
to paralyze his arm. Dancer rained blows on him.

"Coward! To run away from your woman, your child!"

He raised an arm to shield his face from the stinging blows.
Blindly he grabbed Dancer about the waist. For a moment they
swayed, locked together. Then they fell into the rocks, rolling
about.

In silence they fought. Dancer was younger, strong and supple.
But Sam was half a head taller, and heavier. He squeezed hard
with his long arms, feeling Dancer grunt as the air was driven from
him. Propping hands against Sam's chest, Dancer forced him back,
finally got a palm under Sam's chin and drove his head against a
rock. Sam relaxed his grip and Dancer pulled himself free. As he
reached again for his coupstick, fallen among the rocks, Sam caught
at the moccasined leg and pulled him down. The coupstick
snapped.

"Coward!" Dancer panted. "You are not a man!"

Desperately Sam rolled across Dancer's back, drove an elbow
into the youth's head. Dancer's face smashed into a flat slab of rock.
He lay still for a moment, then raised his body on his arms, blood
dripping from the nose. He staggered upright, one hand fumbling
at the knife in his belt.

"Don't!" Sam pleaded. "Friend, don't do it!"

Dancer paused, wiping blood from his face. In the growing light of dawn the blood was a black smear on mouth, hands. "It is better you don't come back then! I guess it is better! If you will not be our medicine, we don't want you to help The People With Hats either!"

Sam took a step backward, but found himself in a cul-de-sac of dawn-lit boulders.

"It is better," Dancer repeated. Picking up the broken coupstick, he examined it. Then he threw it down and stepped toward Sam, knife held low, sharp edge of the blade upmost. Sam remembered the Crow warrior, dead at the Battle of the Rosebud, belly ripped open by a similar knife.

"Wait!" he begged. "Friend, wait!"

Was it going to end this way? Frozen into immobility, Sam watched Dancer approach. Not knowing what else to do, he held out a hand in a placating gesture.

Dancer shook his head. "It is better this way. I see it now. This way is better!"

Crouching, he stalked Sam, moccasins making dark marks in the soft earth that lay among the rocks. Sam pressed back into the boulders. His scrabbling feet found a crevice. He strained upward, back against the rocks, keeping his eye on Dancer. But still he was not out of reach of the knife. Trying to maintain a precarious balance, his groping hand found a shard of granite.

"Stop!" he warned. "Don't come any closer!"

Dancer, knife upraised, lunged; the blade glinted in the light of the rising sun. Desperate, Sam kicked out and the knife spun into the air. Angrily he drove the splinter of stone down hard on Dancer's skull.

Surprised, the young man tottered. He took a step backward, hand fumbling incredulously at his scalplock. Then he fell to one knee, feeling the wound in his head. As Sam watched, his eyes closed; Dancer fell over backward, blood spilling from mouth and ears.

Shaken, Sam got an arm under the youth's shoulders, raised him. "Dancer! I didn't mean to do it!" He wiped the red from the sagging mouth. "Believe me! I—I didn't mean to! Listen to me!"

Dancer's face looked suddenly old. The eyes stared into the rising sun as life drained from them; the body relaxed in Sam's arms.

It was no good. Sam laid him down, got unsteadily to his feet, blinking in the first rays of the sun. As Dancer predicted, the young man had counted coup three times and then died—at Sam Blair's hand. Sam brushed trembling fingers across his mouth, looked down the hill. Noisily the Fat Grass flowed through the shallows, riffles edged with foam. Along the river the great Sioux camp was quiet in the clear light. A pall of smoke lay over the village. But perhaps it was only morning fog rising from the river.

"I'm sorry," Sam muttered. "Goddamn it—I'm sorry!"

For a long time he sat on a bench of rock, gathering strength. After a time, stiffly and painfully he got to his feet. He found the satchel where he had dropped it, and placed it on a flat rock. Picking up Dancer's shattered coupstick, he forced it into the damp earth beside the body. Wearily he carried rocks and piled them over the stiffening form, leaving a small gap so the face could look into a blue and cloudless sky.

Task done, he stood, melancholy, over the makeshift tomb. Wind ruffled the ribbons on the coupstick; the hideous scalps swung to and fro.

"Friend, good-by," he murmured. He made the sign for *farewell:* right hand before his body, back of hand to right, fingers extended, then raising his hand forward and upward, toward the dawn-lit heavens. *Dancer, good-by.*

Climbing upward again, he saw a white face in a cleft in the rocks. The barrel of a rifle glittered in the sun as the trooper sighted down the barrel. Just as the gun went off Sam let out a yell and jumped into the lee of a giant boulder. "Don't shoot!" he begged. "I'm a white man!"

There was silence—all that remained was a distant echo of the shot carroming down the canyon. A startled prairie dog poked his small head from a hole and looked about.

"I'm a white man!" Sam insisted. "Don't shoot! Please!"

Again there was silence. Shortly he heard muttered comment.

"He said he was a white man!"

"I don't care what he said—they're tricky! Shoot the son of a bitch!"

There was another voice then, one with a sound of authority. "Yell down to him! Tell him to come out, with his hands over his head!"

The first voice shouted. "You, down there, whoever you are! Come out from behind that rock, and keep your hands up over your head or I'll blow your guts all over the rocks!"

Obediently Sam stepped from the shelter, hands over his head, black bag dangling high.

"Drop that satchel!" a voice barked.

A bearded trooper with corporal's chevrons watched him. The corporal had a Colt's revolver propped on a rock.

"He don't look like no white man," the corporal reported to someone behind him. "Face and hands black as a nigger!"

Someone else spoke. "Dressed like a damned Sioux, though."

The third voice sounded puzzled. "He ain't got but one moccasin. And see—his foot is plumb white!"

"That's right!" Sam called. "I lost the moccasin when I swam across the river to get away from the Indian camp!"

The corporal stood up, keeping the muzzle of the revolver trained on Sam Blair. "Climb up here, then," he ordered. "And no tricks—hear me?"

Watching Sam clamber awkwardly through the rocks, the corporal asked, "Who in hell are you, anyway?"

Sam paused, wiping perspiration from his brow. "I'm Samuel Penrose Blair," he said. "A physician."

CHAPTER 10

Captain Benteen was suspicious. Crouched behind a barricade of rocks and fallen logs, he looked at Sam Blair.

"A doctor?"

Sam opened his satchel, showed the captain his surgical kit, pills, patent stethoscope. "Springfield Academy of Medicine and Surgery, class of 1869—with honors."

Benteen, whose men had struggled up the hill the previous afternoon to join Major Reno's harried fighters, was heavy-eyed from lack of sleep.

"Then why in hell were you traveling with those Sioux bastards?" The blond mustache twitched as he stared with distrust at Sam. "Dressed like one, too!"

"Look here!" Sam blurted. "You've got plenty of wounded! I can hear them groaning and calling for help! I risked my life to get here! Exactly how and why isn't important! When we get out of this predicament I'll be glad to tell you the whole story! But until then—"

"All right," Benteen conceded. "Hey—Isaacs!"

A lanky corporal in battered felt hat and torn shirt looked up from winding cloth around a bullet gouged arm.

"You're not in fighting condition," Benteen told Isaacs. "I've got another job for you! This man here says he's a doctor. Go round with him and see what he can do for the casualties. But keep an eye on him, you hear, else I'll have your stripes. At the first sign of anything tricky, shoot him dead!"

Sam started to protest the harsh words but bit his tongue. Captain Benteen was tired and in a difficult situation.

"Yes, sir," Isaacs promised. "I'll do 'er, Cap!"

Walking away, Sam offered, "Here—let me help you with that bandage!"

The swarthy corporal held out his arm. "It ain't a bandage," he said. "It's my sergeant's handkerchief; only he ain't gonna blow his nose no more. He took a Sioux arrer through the neck."

In the patchy sunlight filtering through the trees, Sam moved among the wounded, the gaunt Isaacs following him, one hand on the butt of his revolver. That morning Sam stitched up innumerable wounds, extracted broken arrows, gave laudanum to those beyond help. Many times all he could do was pull a blanket over a dead face. Most pressing was the need for water.

"Major sent Lieutenant Smith down the hill with a detail last night," Isaacs said in a dull voice, "but no one came back."

Sam remembered the fight in the tall reeds, a clinking of canteens, the startled voice saying, "He's hit bad! Come over here and help me!"

Shot through the hips, a wounded man grabbed Sam's arm. His lips were cracked, tongue thick. The voice was husky, almost strangled. "Doc, I need water! I got to have water!"

Kneeling, Sam took the small flask of whisky from his satchel. With that terrible wound, the trooper could not last long.

"Water's on the way," he lied. "For now, just have a swig of this! It's whisky—Green River whisky, ninety proof!"

Desperately the man snatched the bottle, held it to his lips, sucking as a baby does a nursing bottle. Some of the precious liquid spilled over the stubbled chin. Sam tried to pull the bottle away but the man's grip was tenacious. Wiping blood from his hands, Sam got to his feet. There hadn't been much left in the flask anyway.

From the valley below, bullets started to lace the boughs over their heads. Cut leaves drifted down and they heard a faraway popping of guns. Corporal Isaacs grabbed Sam's arm and pulled him behind a granite ridge running under the trees like the spine of a prehistoric animal.

"Goddamn it, Doc, keep your head down!"

Sam winced as a spent bullet made a white splash on the granite and dropped near his foot.

"I can't treat the wounded if I skulk here," he protested, and stood up again.

His whisky was gone, the laudanum bottle empty. All that was left was his stock of calomel, blue mass, Dover's Powders, nux vomica, and Blaud's Pills for the anemia. None were useful now. The surgical kit remained; that, a little chloroform, and the stethoscope, though when a man was dead Sam knew it—there was no need to listen. "That soldier over there," he told Isaacs. "The leg is completely destroyed. If you'll help me, I'll cut off what's left and close up the stump. Otherwise, he'll die."

Isaacs was dark, probably Jewish, but he paled.

"Me?"

"You," Sam said. "Stop fingering that damned pistol and give me a hand!"

Major Reno, commanding the troops on the hill, came over and stolidly watched Sam's surgery. "Blair, eh?"

Sam wiped sweat from his forehead. "Yes, sir. Samuel Penrose Blair. I used to practice in Fitch's Landing, down the river."

Reno clenched a ragged stub of cigar between his teeth. He chewed on it, spat out crumbs of tobacco. "I heard that name before someplace. Don't remember where."

The wounded man twitched. Sam gestured to Isaacs. "Drop a little more chloroform on that rag over his nose while I sew up what's left of the leg.

"I don't remember where," Reno repeated. "Well"—he put the cigar stub back in his teeth—"glad you're here, Doctor." He trudged back to the breastworks, propping a worn pair of field glasses on a log to watch the river below.

Near noon, with the sun high overhead, the grove of trees was fetid with heat, with smells of sweat and blood and already-festering wounds. The battle for the hill seemed to have slackened, with only an occasional shot. Sam watched a group of officers gather around Major Reno for a hastily convened council.

"What's happening?" he asked. For a moment he sat down to rest, very tired. Holding out hands before him, he watched them tremble.

"I dunno," Isaacs muttered. "Maybe them red rascals is loading up for one big charge to wipe us out!" Parting the bushes, the corporal looked out at the snow-striped peaks of the Big Horns, far to the south. "Old Crook was supposed to be here by now to help!

And Gin'ral Terry, too!" He slumped beside Sam. "Wonder what's happened to Custer? No one's heard from him since yesterday noon, when he went behind that ridge above the river."

Sam knew what had happened to the flamboyant Custer but said nothing. His throat was dry and cottony and a strange feeling crept over him. Everything seemed distant and detached—sun through the trees, wounded men, scattered canteens and blanket rolls and empty bandoliers—even Corporal Isaacs, elbows propped on knees, a swarm of gnats buzzing around the blood on his arm. It was as if he were looking through the wrong end of a telescope: everything infinitely strange and distant. He was exhausted, light-headed; his head swam. For a moment he closed his eyes. Was he going to faint, for God's sake?

Willing himself to stand, he rose on rubbery legs. "That man over there is delirious," he said to Isaacs. "He's pulled the stitches out of his belly and he's going to bleed to death! Help me to hold him while I try to patch him up again!"

Early in the afternoon someone handed him a piece of hardtack. He chewed it, tried to swallow, but could not get it down. He threw it away, watching a jay snatch it up. The heat in the grove was stifling. Suffering men groaned in pain. What was it old Cump Sherman was supposed to have said? *War is hell!* For a time Sam had been in Sherman's XV Corps.

Hearing a shout, he glanced up. A look-out at the barricade, peering through a telescope, gestured. "Captain Benteen, sir! Come quick!"

Benteen, dirty and disheveled, walked over, accepted the telescope. For a long time he stared down the valley.

"By God," he said in a voice cracked with fatigue, "I believe you're right!"

Rumors began to run round the embattled site. "Something's up!" Isaacs predicted.

Benteen and Major Reno conferred. Junior officers clustered around. A sergeant major joined the group, came back to speak to others of the sergeant hierarchy. The Army, Sam thought wryly, was much the same as it had been at Pea Ridge and Stone's River, so long ago. Corporal Isaacs rose wearily, wincing with pain, and joined a group of corporals. After a while he came back.

"Good news," he reported. "Appears the Sioux are breaking camp and getting ready to travel, though no one knows why!"

Another shout came from the barricade. "Major, here comes Terry! It's General Terry! Look yonder—there ride Terry's men!"

Sam stumbled to the barricade. In the valley below, splashing through the reeds, came mounted men. Guidons fluttered in the wind as others rounded into view.

"Goddamn!" Isaacs exclaimed. "Ain't that a pretty sight, now?"

The column lengthened. Cavalry—more cavalry—hundreds of mounted men. Sam heard the faint music of a bugle. He swallowed and again felt faint. Putting a hand on the barricade, he steadied himself while the defenders cheered.

"The Indians"—his voice broke, and he started again—"the Indians had scouts out. They probably saw Terry and his people. That's why they're leaving."

The beleaguered troopers climbed the barricade and ran down the hill. One group stopped in the brush and a man said, "It's Charlie Reynolds and Bloody Knife!"

Sam looked down at the crumpled figures.

"Charlie was a damned good scout!" someone commented. "And Bloody Knife was a decent man, even if he was a Crow Injun! Many's the time I split a bottle of gin with him at Fort Lincoln!"

Elated, the defenders waded through reeds to greet their rescuers, calling out a profane welcome, shaking hands with friends from the Terry contingent. Men sprawled in the precious water, gulping thirstily. Others filled canteens and carried them up the hill to the wounded. Sam wandered about, clinging to his satchel. Several of the newly arrived troopers looked askance at him in his ragged and torn Sioux clothing. Isaacs reassured them.

"This here is Doc Blair," he explained. "He's a good friend of mine."

A detachment under a downy-cheeked lieutenant of the Third Cavalry galloped down the river to look for General Custer's men. General Terry, worried, sat his horse, fondling a brushy mustache while he talked to Major Reno and Captain Benteen.

"That," Reno concluded, "was the last we saw of them." He nodded to Benteen. "Captain here joined me on the hill with his men around four in the afternoon yesterday. If it hadn't been for that, we'd probably have been wiped out."

Terry dismounted heavily, handed the reins to an orderly.

"No word since then?" he asked.

"Sir, no word since he started around the ridge. Custer might as well be on the moon, as far as we're concerned."

Quickly an interim camp was established along the river. Surgeons from Terry's command set up an operating theater. Sam, weary, introduced himself and set about to help. He was trying to push a spilled gut back into the abdomen when a mournful outcry startled him. The young lieutenant had returned from his search for Custer and his men. Sam wiped blood from his hands, watching the knot of officers.

"All of them," the lieutenant said in a hushed voice.

General Terry was incredulous. "Bradley," he snapped, "don't talk like a damned fool! It can't be!"

Lieutenant Bradley was weeping. He bit his lip, slapped a dusty hat against his thigh.

"It's true!" he insisted. "*All* of them, General! May God be my witness!"

A burly sergeant dismounted. "General, that's true! I hope I never see such a sight again! They're layin' all over the hill up there —cut and scalped and throats slit, private parts—" He shook his head, broke off.

General Terry spoke to Major Reno.

"Marcus, how many men did Custer take up on the ridge with him?"

The major closed his eyes. Swaying a little on his feet, he rubbed his forehead. "Sir," he said. "Let—let me think for a minute."

"There was C Company and E Company," an officer prompted.

"That's right," Reno agreed. "Then there were quite a few from F and I and L."

"How many?" Terry insisted.

Unshed tears lay in Reno's eyes. "A hundred and fifty. Probably more. Say two hundred. Yes, that's about it. Two hundred."

General Terry swore, hit his thigh with a clenched fist. The group around him remained silent, heads bare, staring at the dust. Terry walked away and stood at the edge of the river, chewing his cigar.

"Christ!" a weary surgeon muttered. "Two hundred men!" He shook his head.

In late afternoon Sam sat on a driftwood log at the edge of the river, gazing at lacy foam sparkling with sunbeams. Most of the wounded were patched up, the dead buried. General Terry had sent off a force to pursue the fleeing Indians.

"Dr. Blair? Dr. Samuel Blair?"

Unsteadily he got to his feet. "That's me."

Two officers stood near. They were between him and the sun. To his bloodshot eyes they were silhouettes.

"You're under arrest," a young officer told him.

Sam blinked. His voice was hoarse. "What do you mean?"

He made out the other man, a major with burnished oak leaves. The major was Henry Cushing, from Fort Pike, up the river from Fitch's Landing. Once, a long time ago, Sam had met the saturnine Major Cushing, an Indian fighter of renown, during a summer sociable at the Freeman house. That was where Andy Wyatt met Clara, too, that same night. Major Cushing had left early, but Andy stayed behind to spark Clara.

"I don't understand!" he protested.

Major Cushing's gaze was fixed on the Sioux amulet hanging around Sam's neck; the wakan amulet old Bird Talker, the shaman, had given him.

"Dr. Blair," the major said in a flat voice, "I have to tell you a federal warrant is out for your arrest."

"A—a federal warrant?" Sam faltered. "But—why?"

"On charges of committing treasonable acts against the Government of the United States!"

For a while, Sam was not indicted; everyone was too busy in the aftermath of the Custer massacre. Fuming, the politicians sought a scapegoat. No one suited their purpose exactly. Major Reno and Captain Benteen appeared to have done their best against the horde of Sioux and Cheyenne warriors, and General Custer could not be questioned about the debacle. But in October the Congress finally discovered Samuel Penrose Blair, being held in custody in Major Henry Cushing's guardhouse at Fort Pike and charged with treason.

He was closely guarded and allowed few visitors. One exception was Oscar Roland, reporter for the Chicago *Daily News*. Through the newspaper's connections, Roland managed to visit Sam Blair because of an authorization from the Army's Department of the Missouri. Major Cushing was irate but could not argue with the Department. Roland was a small, dry man with sidewhiskers and a checkered waistcoat. Late one afternoon he brought Sam a box of Cuban *finos* as an introduction. Sam didn't smoke cigars but was grateful for someone to talk to.

"We had better get on solid ground right away," Mr. Roland said, laying bowler hat and cane on the rough wood table. "I'm a reporter on the trail of a big story. You seem a nice fellow, in spite of all the horrible things I'm probably going to write about you. But with me the story comes first."

"I see," Sam murmured.

"The country's gone crazy," Mr. Roland went on, taking the sagging wicker chair. "Men everywhere are signing up to join the Army—the 'Custer Avenger' outfits. Since Sitting Bull and his people split up after the massacre, Crook and Miles have been chasing him all over Hell's half acre. But they can't seem to catch up with him. Some people think the Sioux may be heading for Canada. Once they get across the border, they'll probably be safe."

It was Indian summer. The wooden walls of the guardhouse gave off an oppressive heat where the sun, low in the west, beat on the bleached boards. Sam went to the window and looked out, hoping for a breath of wind. The iron bars were too hot to touch. Dipping a tin cup into the bucket of water, he poured some over his head. Mr. Roland, neat in cravat and tailcoat, appeared too desiccated to sweat.

"Tell me," Sam said. "They whisked me in here so fast I never did find out all that happened at the river."

Roland's small face wrinkled in a grimace. "You're the only person in the whole United States that *don't* know the fine details!" He slapped his pockets, finding a thin sheet of folded newsprint. "Like to keep up on the provincial press! This is the Bismarck *Tribune* for —let me see—yes, the sixth of July last. They claim they were the first to get the story in the papers." He handed the dogeared sheets to Sam, adding, "We picked up the story in Chicago and printed it verbatim—typos and all."

The article was long, taking up the whole front page of the *Tribune*. The headlines were large, black, and dramatic:

MASSACRED!

Gen Custer and 261 Men The Victims

It will be remembered that the Bismark *Tribune* sent a special correspondent with Gen. Terry who was the only professional correspondent with the expedition. Kellogg's last words to the writer were "We leave the Rosebud tomorrow and by the time this reaches you we will have MET and FOUGHT the red devils, with what result remains to be seen. I go with Custer and will be in at the death."

How true! On the morning of the 22nd Gen. Custer took up the line of march for the trail of the Indians reported by Reno on the Rosebud. Gen. Terry, apprehending danger, urged Custer to take additional men, but Custer, having full confidence in his men and in their ability to cope with the Indians in whatever force he might meet them, declined the proffered assistance and marched with his regiment alone. He was instructed to strike the trail of the Indians, to follow it until he discovered their position, and report by courier to Gen. Terry who would reach the mouth of the Little Big Horn by the 26th, when he would act in concert with Custer in the final wiping-out. At four o'clock, the afternoon of the 24th, Custer scouts reported the location of a village recently deserted, whereupon Custer went into camp, marching again at 11 PM, continuing the march until daylight when he again went into camp for coffee. Custer was then fifteen miles from the village located on the Little Horn, one of the branches of the Big Horn, twenty miles above its mouth, which could be seen from the top of the divide, and Gen. Custer pushed on.

The *Tribune* correspondent went on to describe Custer proceeding ". . . with his usual vigor . . ." to find the freshly abandoned Indian camp; probably, Sam thought, the site where Left Hand and his Oglalas camped after the Rosebud fight with Three-Stars Crook.

The article continued with a description of the outbreak of fighting as the troopers met the enemy;

> The Sioux dashed up beside the soldiers, in some instances knocking them from their horses and killing them at their pleasure. This was the case with Lt. McIntosh, who was unarmed except with a saber. He was pulled from his horse, tortured, and finally murdered at the pleasure of the red devils. Frank Girard was separated from the command and lay all night with death and destruction to his comrades within a few feet of him and, but time will not permit us to relate the story, by some means succeeded in saving the fine black stallion in which he took so much pride.

The story described Captain Benteen's arrival to aid the sorely pressed Reno on the hill, and the long wait through the dark hours;

> Near 10 o'clock the fight closed, and the men worked all night strengthening their breastworks, using knives, tincups, and plates in place of spades and picks, taking up the fight again in the morning. In the afternoon of the second day the desire for water became almost intolerable. The wounded were begging piteously for it; the tongues of the men were swollen and their lips parched, and from lack of rest they were almost exhausted. All wondered what had become of Custer.

The piece ended with the arrival of General Terry's troops.

> A panic all at once was created among the Indians and they stampeded, from the hills and from the valleys, and the village was soon deserted except for the dead. Reno and his brave men felt that succor was nigh. Gen. Terry came in sight and strong men wept on each others' necks, but no word was had from Custer. Hand-shaking and congratulations were scarcely over when Lt. Bradley reported that he had found Custer dead, with one hundred and ninety cavalrymen. Imagine the effect! Words cannot picture the feeling of these, his comrades and soldiers. Gen. Terry sought the spot and found it to be true. Of those brave men who followed Custer, all perished; no one lives to tell the story of the battle.

The *Tribune* article ended with a lengthy list of dead and wounded, and asked, "*What Will Congress Do About It? Shall This Be The Beginning Of The End?*"

"Now you know," Roland said.

Sam handed the paper back, but the reporter pushed it toward him, saying, "I guess you haven't seen the little item on page three. It concerns you."

"Concerns me?"

"That's right."

At the bottom of the page was a small item, only a couple of inches of type. It was headed THE MYSTERIOUS HALF-BREED. Unbelieving, Sam read on:

> An officer of Gen. Terry's command reported that during the night of the 26th a half-breed medicine man named Blair deserted the Sioux camp and made his way to the soldiers of Major Reno's command on the hill above the river. The circumstances are suspicious, and it is understood the man is being held on charges of being one of Sitting Bull's spies, attempting to sow mischief among the valiant and hard-pressed soldiers.

Roland grinned. "They got it all wrong, of course! I suppose it *could* be said you're a kind of medicine man, though! Anyway, my *Daily News* got it right. Now you're charged with taking up arms against Cushing's troopers last winter, in the snow. You're also charged with giving aid and comfort to the enemy—the Sioux, that is—at the Battle of the Rosebud. I expect the federal prosecutor in Omaha is working up an indictment that you planned the whole Custer massacre yourself!"

"Treason," Sam murmured, unbelieving. "That's what they're going to call it. Treason! I don't know anyone less treasonable than I am! I'm a doctor, that's all! I help sick and hurt people no matter what the color of their skin! Is that treason?"

"Probably is," Roland said. "Do you know the definition of treason?"

"No."

"You ought to have a lawyer!"

"They're getting me one, I understand, but I haven't seen him yet."

"Well," Roland said, "treason is defined in the U. S. Codes like this." He read from a notebook. "'Whoever, owing allegiance to the United States, levies war against them or adheres to their enemies, giving them aid and comfort, within the United States or elsewhere, is guilty of treason.'"

Sam put his head in his hands. "I guess that covers me."

Roland reached for hat and cane. "You be honest with me, Samuel Blair, and I'll be honest with you. I don't think you've got the chance of a pig in a sausage factory. The Army is looking for a scapegoat in the Custer thing, and you're all they can lay their hands on. Back east they're blowing up a storm. The Secretary of War and the Attorney General already put their heads together and decided you'll do nicely for a sacrificial lamb." He adjusted his cravat, dabbed thin lips with a handkerchief. "Actually, I think it's a hard case for them to make, given normal times. A good defense attorney would shoot them full of holes. But these aren't normal times! The nation wants revenge!"

The guard rattled the bars of Sam's cell. "Time's up, Mr. Roland! And there's a lady waiting to see the prisoner."

Sam rose. "A lady?"

"I'll be back to talk to you in more detail tomorrow," Roland promised. He looked around the cramped cell with distaste, poked a dirty tin plate with his cane, wrinkled his nose. "The *News* is a big paper. It has influence even out here, at the end of creation. I'll see what I can do to help you, Sam. All you have to do is tell me your personal story."

Sam went to the bars. "A lady?"

Roland nodded farewell, departed.

"A Mrs. Freeman," the guard explained.

Sam's heart leaped up. Clara? No, it couldn't be Clara! She had gone to Washington with Andy Wyatt. Besides, the guard had said Mrs. Freeman, not Mrs. Wyatt.

"Ten minutes, ma'am—no more," the guard cautioned, and let Clara's mother into the cell to throw her arms about Sam.

"Oh, Sam!" she wept. "How can they do this to you? I know you couldn't do anything wrong!"

Gently he disengaged her, offered the wicker chair. He sat on a stool opposite.

"I—I'm glad you were able to come, ma'am."

"I *demanded* to see you!" she said indignantly. "I told Henry Cushing it was cruel and inhuman to keep you penned up this way without anyone to talk to!" She folded arms over an ample bosom in satisfaction. "After all, I know a few things about Henry! I give him a piece of my mind!"

"Henry Cushing would love to hang me himself," Sam said dourly.

"We were all trying to get in to see you," she went on. "Ma Bidwell, Joe Harris, Jacob Almayer, even Bertha Rambouillet and her girls! They kind of elected me chairman, I guess you could say, and I come out here with fire in my eye!" She eyed him. "You're so thin! Are they feeding you enough? Henry finally give in and said I could bring you potpie and cookies and things if you wanted. And those clothes—that old shirt and those dirty pants! I could do laundry for you, or maybe I could find some of the mister's old pants. And Clara said—"

"Clara?"

Mrs. Freeman wiped her eyes, blew her nose. "She's here, Sam! Come out on the cars!"

"But Clara and Andy Wyatt—"

"I know," Mrs. Freeman sighed. "I don't think Clara's too happy. Andy's busy at the War Department, and Clara don't know anybody in Washington. Andy's pa is rich, you know. He give them a big house in Rock Creek Park—that's somewheres near Washington—and Clara's supposed to dress up all the time and entertain the bigwigs; generals and politicians and ambassadors and like that."

"I thought that's what she wanted!"

"Wanting and having is two different things," Mrs. Freeman explained. "Clara always thought she'd enjoy fooforaw like that, but when the time come it wasn't so nice. Andy always wanted her to dance with a congressman or have tea with the general's wife, and she didn't hardly have him to herself at all, the way she thought." She leaned forward and tapped his knee. "My Clara is really a simple girl, Sam! She just ain't cut out for such as that. Her and Andy already had words about it."

"But why did she come all the way out here?"

"I dunno, exactly," Mrs. Freeman admitted. "She *said* she was homesick, told Andy she just had to see her ma or she'd pine away. So he give her the money and she come."

"I see," Sam murmured.

"Anyway," Mrs. Freeman went on, "she didn't want to come out to the post with me. I begged her, but she said it didn't look right with Andy and her having trouble and you used to be sweet on her once." She fumbled in her reticule. "Clara did say to give you this, though." She handed him a small envelope with a richly embossed legend in one corner: CAPTAIN AND MRS. ANDREW AYLESWORTH WYATT.

"Andy made captain already?"

Mrs. Freeman nodded. "Passed him over a passel of other officers, though Clara give me to understand it was his pa's money bought it for him. Oh, well—"

"Time's up!" called the guard.

She opened the small watch dangling between her ample breasts. "Guess I got to go now."

He escorted her to the iron door. "Thanks for coming," he said. "It's been lonesome."

She bussed him on the cheek, again wrapped plump arms about him. "Now just don't you worry, Sam! Everything is going to come out all right. You couldn't do a mean thing if you had to!" She hesitated, fumbled with her reticule. "You was always my favorite, anyway! I dunno why Clara picked that stuck-up Andy Wyatt!"

After she left, he hurriedly opened the envelope. It was dusk, but the walls radiated heat. He heard the faint whisper of a bugle. *Soupy, soupy, soupy!* That meant mess call. Soon they would bring him beans and salt beef, a cup of sour-tasting coffee, dry bread or hardtack. Impatient, he spread out the note.

Sam, I've made a big misteak but maybe it isn't too late to make it up to you somehow, anyway I can. Andy says they're going to hang you but I know there's a chance. I've got money from Andy though he doesn't know it. I made arrangements to get you a lawyer from Omaha. Be of good cheer, like it says in a book I read once you lent me.

It was signed, "Love, Clara."

Standing at the barred window, he watched the western sky dissolve into swirls of pink and green and yellow. Another bugle call came from the parade ground, one he didn't recognize. When a breath of air stirred he leaned his forehead against the bars to take advantage of it. From the corridor he heard the rattle of tin as a soldier brought his evening meal.

Clara, he thought. *Clara Freeman!* No, it was Clara Wyatt, now, Mrs. Captain Andrew Aylesworth Wyatt, of Rock Creek Park. He was surprised at the clarity of the vision that came to him. Though it had been nearly a year, his mind's eye saw in the sky the yellow hair in ringlets, the eyes, cornflower blue, and the searching way they watched him that night in town, when she told him she was going to marry Andy Wyatt. Her chin—he remembered the delicate cleft, the way her lip trembled. *Sam, I never meant to hurt you! You're a fine man, and I'll always think of you with admiration and respect! But Andy is offering me so much more!* Now it hadn't worked out.

He was standing there, watching the dying day, when tattoo sounded. For a long time Clara Freeman had been absent from his thoughts. Now she had returned, a powerful and disturbing presence. But he—Sam Blair—was charged with treason and likely to hang for it.

CHAPTER 11

The trial of Samuel Penrose Blair was held in Federal Court, Omaha, starting the afternoon of the twenty-sixth of December, 1876, the day after Christmas. The judge was Matthew Cleary, a white-haired giant of a man, impressive in dark robes. After a seemingly endless series of pretrial motions, none of which Judge Cleary granted, the trial began.

Jesse Emmett, the lawyer whom Clara had obtained, leaned across the table and whispered, "Cleary's a fair man, Sam; well-respected on the bench." Emmett himself was originally from Boston, but had come west for his lungs.

The U. S. Attorney was much younger than Jesse Emmett. His name was Horace Waddell. In spite of his relative youth he had established a reputation as an up-and-coming prosecutor. "Probably be governor of the state someday," Mr. Emmett opined.

In spite of bad weather, the snow drifting down on an accumulation already a foot or more deep, the court was crowded. Newspaper reporters, military men, and politicians thronged the halls of the Federal Building, along with curiosity-seekers. The big room smelled of worn boards, tobacco smoke, and human bodies. Clara and her mother, through Jesse Emmett, had seats near the wooden railing separating the court proper from spectators. Sam was surprised and touched to see old friends from Fitch's Landing in the audience: Charlie Daigle, Jacob Almayer—even Bertha Rambouillet with one of her girls. All were poor; he wondered how they had financed the trip to the city. Jake Almayer was poverty-stricken as any church mouse. Yet there was Jake, in celluloid collar and dusty black coat, sitting in a back row, hat clutched in work-worn hands.

Selection of the jury took a long time. Jesse Emmett and Waddell sparred for the best people to support their case. On the hard chair Sam squirmed, wondering why Emmett challenged this juror; Waddell, that one. All of the panel seemed pleasant and fair-minded. "Why did you turn down that fellow in the pince-nez?" he asked. "The one worked at the bank?"

Emmett smiled dryly. "Didn't you hear him say his son was in the Army? Ninth Infantry?"

Sam shook his head. He had been too busy watching Clara. She was pale but stylish in a hat with peacock feathers and what he once heard called a "paletot"—a kind of velvet coat with long sleeves and a high neck, buttoning down the front. In provincial Omaha, Clara was the object of admiring stares.

"The Ninth Infantry," Emmett explained, "is presently chasing Sitting Bull somewhere in the Big Horns. That bank clerk would give you short shrift."

At last Prosecutor Waddell got to his feet. The judge nodded and the young man cleared his throat for the opening statement. He proposed to show, clearly and without doubt, that Samuel Blair, a physician of Springfield, Missouri, and later of Fitch's Landing, on the Yellowstone, had committed treasonable acts against the Government of the United States. "In a time like this," Waddell said in a rich baritone, hooking thumbs under his lapels, "when the nation reels under the impact of the savage slaughter at the Little Big Horn, June twenty-fifth last, the public must be made aware there are evil white men about, traitors to their country, who aided and abetted the savage Sioux in their depredations, rapine, and murder, setting to the torch the dwellings of peaceable settlers on Government lands. Such malefactors have taken up arms against the peaceful expansion of these great United States into the western regions. The nation—nay, the *world*—must understand that a Government of the people, by the people, and for the people cannot stand idly by and see such rascals work their mischief!"

Emmett tapped a pencil impatiently. "Swill," he grumbled. "But skillful swill! Look how the jury's eating it up!"

Sam's throat turned dry and parched as he heard himself described as wicked, brutish, and pagan in nature. At the end of his statement Sam was uneasy. "They might as well get a rope right now and put an end to all this," he muttered. "What chance have I got?"

Emmett grinned, clapped him on the back. "Waddell is a pompous ass! That kind of blather listens fine but it's like spun-sugar candy at a county fair—chew on it a while and you've got nothing left." In response to Judge Cleary's nod he rose.

"Your honor, gentlemen of the jury, my distinguished colleague in the halls of justice—Mr. Horace Waddell—citizens who have taken time to attend this momentous trial—"

To Sam Blair that sounded also like sugar candy, quick to melt in the mouth and leave no trace. His attention wandered, and he saw Jake Almayer raise a hand almost imperceptibly in salute; he nodded. Bertha Rambouillet, splendid in high-piled red hair and flower-studded hat, smiled at him and nudged one of her girls, a lanky snub-nosed child whom Sam remembered treating for bronchitis two winters ago. Charlie Daigle, the livery-stable proprietor from Fitch's Landing, smiled encouragingly and old Mrs. Freeman winked in an absurd, heavy-lidded gesture. Beside her sat Clara, gloved and formally gowned, an expensive fur coat—probably from one of Washington's smart shops on the Avenue—thrown carelessly open, held in position only by a gold chain across her bosom. Face pale, she stared unwinking at Sam, blue eyes large and uneasy.

"Eh?" At the sound of his name Sam turned.

"I say," lawyer Emmett repeated with some annoyance, "that there is no legitimate way this court can find Samuel Penrose Blair guilty of *anything*, let alone the absurd charge of treason! I am pained that all the panoply of the federal courts must be called into play to harass this innocent physician, whose only motive was to relieve the distress of fellow human beings."

Someone catcalled from a back row: "Sioux ain't no human beings!"

There was widespread chuckling but Emmett was unruffled.

"In conclusion, may it please the court, I must say I have every confidence in the fairness and humanity of this select jury. Which of them has not called on the man of medicine to relieve his sufferings, succor wife and children in pain and illness, act as understanding friend and counselor in time of crisis? Now, gentlemen, it is your turn to requite the debt all humanity owes to the unselfish practitioners of the blessed art of healing!"

There was meager and scattered applause. Judge Cleary frowned and tapped his gavel in warning.

"Mr. Waddell, you may introduce the Government's first witness."

Sam was startled to see the face of the *slota* half-breed, the trader from the Red River country who had visited Left Hand's village in winter, bearing an order from the Army for the Sioux to come in to the Standing Rock reservation.

In halting English, heavily accented, Louis Moreau told his story. He had seen Sam at the Oglala camp.

"What was his role there?" Waddell asked.

Moreau looked puzzled.

"I mean—how was he regarded by the Indians?"

Moreau scratched his head. "He dress like Indian. He act like Indian. He talk like Indian!"

"When you presented the Army's order to Left Hand, the Oglala chief, where was Dr. Blair?"

"By damn, he sit right in with them—with all the chief and Strong Hearts and Bad Faces and the big men! Like he one of them!"

"Thank you," Waddell said.

Emmett cross-examined.

"What was Dr. Blair doing there, in that council?"

"Eh?"

"He just sat there, didn't he? Didn't speak or anything? Wasn't he just an observer?"

Moreau agreed. "He just sit there."

"Didn't carry weapons, didn't do a war dance or whoop or act hostile in any way?"

Moreau looked at Waddell. The prosecutor turned away, examined his notes.

"No," Moreau admitted. "He just sit there. Listen."

"Thank you," Emmett said. "You may step down."

The next witness for the prosecution was a young man with a crippled arm. He wore an ill-fitting gray suit, but the shoes were shined to perfection.

"Your name?" Waddell asked.

"John Kelly, sir. Formerly of B Company, Third Cavalry." It was the trooper Sam Blair treated during the Rosebud fight, the young trumpeter with the broken arm.

"You were with General Crook's forces on June eighteenth last at the Rosebud battle?"

"Yes, sir."

"What was Dr. Blair doing?"

"Well, sir, I took a ball through my arm—" Kelly held up the injured member. "I was laying against the cliff, and this Indian—at least, he looked like a Sioux, was dressed like one, and had long braided hair and all—he come down the canyon and fixed up my arm. He had a satchel like a doctor, but at first I was scared. I figured he was going to kill me. Then he spoke English. He said 'I'm white as you are.' He set my arm and stitched it up and put splints on it. If it wasn't for that—"

"Thank you, Corporal," Waddell interrupted. "But I'm more interested in what happened later."

Kelly rubbed his forehead. "I was kind of dizzy from the stuff he gave me to kill the pain—opium, I think it was. But I remember there was some Sioux come dashing by and run up the canyon to set up a defensive position in the rocks. This Indian—Dr. Blair, I mean—joined the Sioux and retreated up the canyon with them."

Waddell nodded. "So he went with the Sioux, the people that had just been fighting General Crook's column!"

"Yes, sir—that's right. But—"

"Your witness," Waddell told Mr. Emmett.

"No questions," Sam's lawyer said.

Young Kelly looked at the judge. When Judge Cleary gestured, he rose slowly, almost undecided, and stepped from the box.

It was getting late. The judge adjourned court until the following day. Sam was escorted across Florence Street to the jail by armed guards. He caught a quick glimpse of gunmetal sky, hurrying passersby, heads down against a rising wind, before he was taken back to his cell. As a federal prisoner he received better fare than at Fort Pike. Eating fried pork chops and applesauce brought from a nearby restaurant, he asked lawyer Emmett, "Why didn't you cross-examine Kelly?"

Emmett sipped coffee, bit the end from a stogie.

"Didn't need to! Everybody in that courtroom knew you'd fixed up the boy's arm, maybe saved him from an amputation. Kelly was grateful, too—tried to say so, but Waddell wouldn't let him. No, the point had been made! It would be foolish to stir up any other reaction from young Kelly. After all, it was a Sioux ball that broke his arm, wasn't it? He can't think kindly of them."

Next day, Major Henry Cushing was the first witness. He was sworn in and sat easily in dress blues, the model of a longtime Army professional. After preliminary questioning, Waddell said, "Describe now, if you will, Major, how you found Dr. Blair when General Terry's relief column arrived."

Cushing sat straight as a ramrod, hat in lap, booted legs crossed.

"Sir, I had been aware of Dr. Blair's defection—"

"Objection!" Emmett got to his feet.

"On what grounds, Mr. Emmett?" Judge Cleary asked.

"Defection is an onerous word, sir. The fact has yet to be proven in this court."

Judge Cleary nodded. "Sustained."

Major Cushing began again. "I—I had been aware that Dr. Blair was accused—let me say, *suspected*—of having given aid and comfort to the Sioux, even taken up arms against our cavalry units. I knew also there was a warrant out for his arrest, based on a statement by one of my soldiers that he had observed Dr. Blair in the camp of the notorious Sioux warrior Left Hand, on the occasion of an action by my troops last winter. Therefore, when I rode in with General Terry on June 26 and saw Dr. Blair in full Indian garb, I was puzzled. I brought the matter up to General Terry, and he authorized me to place Dr. Blair under arrest."

"There is more," Waddell urged. "You spoke to me about a necklace—a kind of amulet on a cord."

"Yes, sir," the major agreed. "I have been fighting Indians on the frontier since '57, when I was with General Harney at Bear Butte. I know the Sioux and the Cheyennes well, and their characteristics and customs. There is among the Sioux a warrior society known as the Strong Hearts. The amulet Dr. Blair wore is their official—well, call it a badge of office."

"What is the further significance of the amulet?"

"It is given," Major Cushing testified, "only to men who perform some conspicuous act of bravery in battle. In fact, the Strong Hearts are composed only of the best warriors. No one can join the Strong Hearts—their membership is very limited—unless he is an accomplished warrior and has taken a lot of scalps."

Sam pushed back his chair.

"That's not true!" he protested. "I mean—I didn't do anything brave! Bird Talker was the medicine man! He just gave me that thing, that necklace, because we were friends! I didn't even know—"

"Silence!" Judge Cleary pounded his gavel.

"But—"

Emmett grabbed Sam's arm, pulled him down. "Be quiet! I'll tell you when to talk!"

Judge Cleary peered over steel-rimmed spectacles.

"Dr. Blair, this is a court of law! There is a procedure specified for conduct of defendant and witness, prosecutor and counsel. I must tell you such outbreaks can be prejudicial to your case." He laid the gavel down. "Major, you may proceed."

"Sir," Cushing said, "that's about all I had to say, I think."

Emmett then cross-examined. "What was Dr. Blair doing when the relief column arrived?"

Major Cushing stroked the brim of the hat lying in his lap. "He was sitting along the river, just—kind of staring into the water."

"But what *had* he been doing, before?"

"Well," Cushing said, "I understand he had been treating Major Reno's wounded. Yes, that is a fact. Both Major Reno and Captain Benteen told me that."

"So," Emmett concluded, "it was also a fact that he escaped from the Indian camp, swam across the river, and joined Major Reno's forces, even after being shot at by them, to perform a humane function of treating the wounded."

Cushing hesitated.

"Is that not correct, sir?" Emmett insisted.

"Yes, I suppose so."

"He was, then, acting as a physician, a man bound by the oath of the Greek physician Hippocrates to treat all sufferers alike, regardless of race, creed, color, or anything else? That is a paraphrase of Hippocrates, but essentially accurate."

Cushing murmured, "Yes, sir. I have read that oath."

"Thank you, Major," the lawyer said.

Court was dismissed until one in the afternoon. The snow was falling heavier; Omaha was blanketed. Sam, given a tray with boiled beef and noodles, looked askance at it. "My stomach's been acting up," he told Emmett. "It's been a long time since I ate white man's food. Maybe I'm not used to it. Or maybe it's just the pressure, the"—he swallowed—"the uncertainty."

Emmett put a hand on his shoulder. "You're in a tight spot. I told you that already, Sam. But trials like this sometimes take strange turns, and I'm doing all I can to produce some of those unexpected turns. Trust me!"

Sam picked at the food. "I've got to trust you," he sighed, "and I'm really thankful I've got a good lawyer. Nevertheless, it seems like I'm eating just about my last meal. You know, the condemned man—"

"You're not condemned yet," Emmett reassured him. He fished in an inside pocket. "By the way, here's something Mrs. Wyatt asked me to pass to you."

Sam read the note:

Dear Sam:

Mama and I pray for you every night in the hotel. I think things are going well. Mr. Emmett says you are berring up well, though mama thinks you look peaked. Don't worry too much, because I know everything is going to come out all right. We both send our love. Clara.

There was a postscript.

Andy sent me a telegraphic message to come home. But I'm staying till you're aquited.

Clara never was a good speller. Sam folded the note, put it in his pocket. A faint scent—perfume? That was a habit she must have picked up in Washington.

"Thanks," he told Emmett. "How is she? I mean—how does she look? Is she all right?"

Emmett lit a fresh stogie. "She and her mother are worried, of course. That's understandable. But her confidence in you is unshakable." He peered at Sam through blue-gray clouds of smoke. "You know her very well?"

"I—we—that is, we were engaged, once. Or almost engaged. Then she married another man, a cavalry lieutenant. They live back in Washington."

On the way back to the courtroom, flanked by guards, Sam met Oscar Roland, shawl tied over bowler hat, jumping nimbly out of the way of an oncoming dray wagon.

"Been busy at the telegraph office all morning, sending copy to the paper. How are you?"

Sam shook his head. "Not so good. Stomach bothers me."

Nose red with cold, the little man pressed his arm. "After hearing what you went through, I guess I'm on your side now. Anyway, I kind of leaned that way in the final chapter, though most people I've talked to think you're guilty as Cain!"

The final chapter. Sam felt a chill not entirely owing to the weather.

"There's a lot of folks reading your story," Roland went on. "We're running it in installments. Circulation's increased by ten thousand copies a day! It's driving the rest of the Chicago papers crazy!" He waved to Sam as the guards pulled him away. "Good luck!"

That afternoon a waterpipe broke in an overhead office and flooded the courtroom. Judge Cleary adjourned court until the damage could be repaired. Sam lay sleepless in his cell. Things were coming to a head. The prosecution, confident, had announced only one more witness.

A lamp in the corridor cast a black grillwork on the wall as it shone through the bars. He could smell the thick stench of coal oil. The turnkey, sitting on a chair cocked against the wall, snored. From far away, muffled by the falling snow, Sam heard a bell toll. Midnight? Wide-eyed, hands clasped behind his head, he stared upward into blackness.

After a while images formed on the ceiling. A village, an Indian village. Circles of lodges—the Sioux liked things that were round. The sun was round, the moon was round, their war drums were round, villages were laid out in a circle. Round. Round. As in the circular lens of a telescope, he saw a scene on the dark ceiling. People came and went; they cooked, sewed, had children, hunted. He heard singing. The Sioux sang a great deal. Sweet Grass Woman had a soft sweet voice, very gentle. It lulled him—he became drowsy.

What? he asked, making the gesture: fingers raised in the air and pointed in several directions. *What? What song are you singing?*

It was not a happy song. This melody was in a minor key—a descending figure, mournful. He opened his eyes and looked at her.

What is wrong?

Slowly she came toward him. He raised on an elbow, curious.

What is that you have?

Sweet Grass Woman's eyes were large and sad. She carried a bundle in her arms, a small bundle wrapped in a square cut from a trade blanket. Instantly he knew what it was.

The baby.

Yes.

Is it—is it well?

As she came toward him, her figure grew larger and she held out the bundle.

Yes. It is well.

Is there—does it have a name?

The form grew larger, filling the ceiling. The blanket-wrapped bundle bore down on him; he shrank back.

Yes. There is a name.

Sweet Grass Woman's voice, always soft and well-modulated, was very loud. He wondered why the guard didn't hear. Her form now extended beyond the boundaries of the ceiling. The blanket-wrapped bundle filled the space, pressing down, smothering him. He called out in panic.

"No! Please! No!"

"Sam?"

Clutching the straw-filled pillow, he opened his eyes.

"Sam! It's me—Emmett! What's the matter?"

Gasping, he sat up. Milky daylight streamed from the barred window. He was cold, and shivered. Lawyer Emmett and the guard watched him.

"What's wrong?" Emmett demanded. "You were yelling and rolling around and kicking!"

Dazed, Sam sat on the edge of the cot, holding the pillow in his arms. He took a deep breath, stood up shakily.

"I—I'm all right," he stammered. "I guess it was just a dream. A bad dream."

The final prosecution witness was Luther Speck, the young German corporal Sam had once treated for the scabies in Fitch's Landing. Speck sat nervously in the witness chair, not looking at Sam Blair. He gave his name and rank; then Prosecutor Waddell led him through his story.

"It was winter—yes? What month?"

"December," Luther said. "December sixteenth."

The Moon When Deer Shed Their Horns. Sam remembered going out to cut the Christmas tree.

"Tell us about the attack."

Luther swallowed hard. "I guess the Sioux thought they were safe, the snow being so deep. We found a look-out, and one of the civilian scouts killed him with a knife before he could move. Maybe he was asleep, I don't know. Then we rode right into the camp, yelling and shooting. We caught them off guard." He gazed around, wet lips with his tongue. His glance fell on Sam but he looked quickly away.

"Did you shoot anyone?" Waddell asked.

"Yes."

"Only one, you told me."

"Yes."

"Do you remember that man, the one you shot?"

"Yes, sir. I—do."

"What was that man doing?"

Luther swallowed, Adam's apple bobbing up and down in a freshly shaven throat. "Well, he was a Sioux. At least, I thought he was a Sioux. He was dressed like all the rest."

"What was he *doing?*" Waddell insisted.

Luther hesitated. "He—he was fighting us, like the others."

"You saw him fighting against the soldiers of Major Cushing's command?"

"Yes, sir."

"Expand a little, if you please."

"What?"

Waddell's voice was impatient. "Just tell us what the man was doing! Firing a gun?"

"First," Luther said, "I saw him fighting with Billy Harmon, Private Harmon. Billy had just run his saber through a Sioux, and this other man—"

"Dr. Blair?" Waddell asked. "The defendant?"

Luther's face twisted in passion. "He was a good man! He was the kindest man I ever knew! Many's the time he helped me, did something for me when I needed it! He helped Ma get her pension! He—"

Judge Cleary's gavel tapped the dark wood.

"I don't care!" Luther insisted. "He'd never do anything wrong! He ain't that kind of a man! Why don't you ask him how he come to be there, do what he done?"

"Silence!" Judge Cleary cautioned. "Young man, I will hold you in contempt of court if you continue!"

Abashed, Luther sank back in the chair, gnawing at his knuckles. "I'm sorry," he murmured.

The judge's gavel sounded again to still a buzz of comment that ran round the courtroom. Sam saw Mr. Roland scribbling in his notebook.

"Mr. Waddell," Judge Cleary said, "please continue."

Waddell bowed, adjusted the chain spanning his vest. "Thank you, Your Honor." He turned to the reluctant witness.

"Now, Corporal, I must ask you again! The defendant, Samuel Blair, dressed as a Sioux, was doing what?"

Luther took a deep breath. "He was wrassling with Billy Harmon. Took Billy's saber away."

"What did Billy do then?"

"He got away from there. But another Sioux run up behind Billy and stuck him with a lance. That was all. Billy just—dropped."

"And then?"

"Billy and me was good friends. I rode after the Sioux had the lance, but he dodged behind a tree. The other man was standing there, waving Billy's saber. So I turned Malcolm A. on him—that's my horse—to ride him down. Just as I come up on him he raised the saber, maybe to protect himself—"

"Don't speculate, Corporal," Waddell cautioned. "Just say what happened!"

"I looked down the barrel of my carbine and saw it was Dr. Blair. I didn't want to pull the trigger! I tried not to, but it was too late! The gun went off, and he fell down."

There was silence in the courtroom. After a pause to regain his composure, Luther resumed his story.

"There was a lot of Sioux milling around, and they started shooting from behind rocks and places. So the trumpeter blew recall and we stopped burning tipis and things and rode away." He took a shuddering breath. "That's—that's all."

"One final question," Waddell said. "Is it your opinion that the defendant, Dr. Blair, was actually fighting as a Sioux? That is to say, bearing arms against federal troops?"

"Objection!" Emmett snapped. "You can't ask for an opinion!"

"Then I'll rephrase my question," Waddell said. "Corporal, in your experience as a military man, was Dr. Blair actually bearing arms against you and your fellow soldiers?"

Luther looked at Sam. His hands gripped the oaken arms of the chair.

"Corporal, please answer!"

Speck remained silent, looking at fingers clamped on the chair.

"Your Honor," Waddell said, "Please direct the witness to answer the question!"

Luther's lip trembled. He bit down hard to still the quivering. Judge Cleary reached for his gavel.

"Young man, I warn you that you are required to answer Mr. Waddell's question now—right now—on pain of disciplinary action."

Luther pounded his fists on the chair, agonized. Sam could stand it no longer. He rose.

"Tell the truth, Luther! It's all right!"

The young man's eyes filled with tears. He swung his head like a cornered animal.

"It's all right!" Sam insisted.

With bowed head, Luther answered. "Yes. I guess he did."

The prosecutor smiled. "Cross-examine!" he invited Sam's lawyer.

"Only one question, Luther," Emmett murmured. His face was

thoughtful as he paced the worn boards, hands clasped behind his back. "Actually, you did not see Dr. Blair strike anyone, shoot anyone, kill anyone?"

Luther's voice was eager. "No! All he did was grab Billy Harmon's saber!"

"After that he just stood there?"

Luther nodded. "Like he was kind of dazed!"

Mr. Emmett smiled.

"Thank you, young man," he said. "You may step down."

Crossing Florence Street to the jail, Sam said to Emmett, "Why didn't you ask Luther anything else? Seems to me it was a pretty short cross-examination!"

"No need—the boy had already made you out a sympathetic character! Just let me handle the tactics! Maybe this was the unexpected happening I spoke of!"

Nevertheless, a man hurled a snowball in Sam's face as he entered the jail. "Move on, you!" a guard growled. But a woman spat at Sam, and a gang of boys shouted in chorus, "Indian lover! Indian lover!"

The snowball had had a rock in it. Sam's lip bled so, he could not eat the stew the turnkey brought. There was something else that killed his appetite. In spite of lawyer Emmett's easy assurances, he did not feel that being made out a sympathetic character was going to do him any good. Maybe Benedict Arnold had been a sympathetic character too, but that made Arnold no less a traitor to the United States. If he had not escaped to the British, Arnold would have hanged. But Sam Blair had no place to escape to.

CHAPTER 12

Sam had no witnesses for his defense. In vain Mr. Emmett tried to subpoena both Major Reno and Captain Benteen to testify Sam had been of inestimable value in treating the wounded on the hill above the Little Big Horn. The Army, however, declared the officers too deeply engaged in military operations to be spared. Cletus Wiley, who might have testified to the validity of Sam's claim that he had been virtually a prisoner in the Oglala camp and had tried to escape, could not be found; he was probably visiting one of his Indian wives. Many of Sam's old friends from Fitch's Landing wanted to testify to Sam's good character, but Emmett did not believe they would be useful.

"We need to convince the jury you were a creature of circumstance—that what happened to you was against your will and couldn't be helped! When I put you on the stand tomorrow, we'll sail in that direction." Emmett was a frustrated sailor, now landlocked in Omaha.

The next day, the lawyer led Sam carefully through a thicket of questions.

"The Indians seized you, then, on the old Military Road and took you to Left Hand's camp."

"That's right."

"Why?"

"It's my belief they thought I could cure the chief's crippled hand. But the surgery was far beyond anyone's ability."

"And with the use of your Magnetic Tractors you impressed them to the extent they spared you."

"That's right."

"Shortly after, you tried to escape."

Sam nodded. "They came after me, though, and brought me back."

"When the soldiers attacked Left Hand's camp in the dead of winter, you did not attack any of them?"

"No, sir," Sam said.

"Corporal Speck testified you took a saber away from a trooper."

"I did. But I was only trying to stop the killing. The Oglalas had been surprised, and there were women and children, innocent people, who were in danger of being killed."

There was a murmur from the audience, but a frown from Judge Cleary brought silence. Emmett went on, trying to picture Sam Blair as a helpless pawn.

"At the Battle of the Rosebud you did not carry arms of any kind?"

"No, sir. Nothing but my satchel, my physician's satchel with its surgical kit and medicines."

"Your only purpose was to treat the wounded?"

"Yes, sir."

Emmett contemplated the jury. "Gentlemen, that seems to me to be a humane purpose—a very humane purpose."

Judge Cleary interrupted. "Mr. Emmett, I don't understand where this line of questioning is leading us. What are you trying to establish?"

Emmett bowed. "Your Honor, if you will allow me to continue, I think the purpose of my questioning will become evident to Your Honor, and to these fair-minded jurymen."

"Well, then—" Judge Cleary settled back.

"Now." Emmett paced the worn boards. "At the battle of the Little Big Horn—"

"Objection!" prosecutor Waddell interrupted.

The judge peered over his spectacles. "On what grounds, sir?"

"It was not a battle! It was a massacre! The public press has consistently referred to it as such! The Army speaks of it in those terms! The public knows it as a massacre! After all, when a handful of brave soldiers is overwhelmed by thousands of ruthless savages—"

Judge Cleary pounded his gavel.

"Mr. Waddell, don't try to inflame the jury by intemperate remarks! The matter is under intensive investigation by congressional committees, as well as by the Army and other agencies. For the moment, we must call it a battle!"

Sulky, Waddell sat down. Sam's lawyer resumed his questioning.

"At the actual battle, you did not participate?"

"No, sir. They kept me locked up, with a guard."

"Why was that?"

"They were afraid I would escape and take some word of the Indian strength, or their disposition, to the soldiers."

"Ah!" Emmett said, as if surprised by an important development.

"After the battle they were all celebrating. No one was watching me, so I got away, swam the river, and went up the hill to Major Reno's command." Sam did not mention the tragic encounter with Dancer. Perhaps it might help his case to testify he had to fight his way to Reno's position, but that seemed a private matter.

"While you were in the Indian camp," Emmett continued, "I understand you kept a daily journal. What was in that journal, or diary, sir?"

"I kept a record of everything that happened to me. It had details of my capture, of my attempt to escape. There was a lot about the Rosebud fight and how I treated the wounded on both sides."

There was a muffled catcall from the audience. When Judge Cleary made a tentative motion toward the gavel the disturbance subsided.

"I understand that this journal, which might do much to establish your position as a prisoner, a helpless prisoner, was unfortunately left behind when you fled the Indian camp."

"That's right. I couldn't carry much."

"Your Honor," Emmett said, turning to the judge, "I have shown that Dr. Blair did the best he could in a desperate situation. He acted with honor, and with full acknowledgment of his obligations as a citizen of these United States." He cast his gaze on the jury. "You gentlemen would very likely have done the same thing, given the same circumstances. A charge of treason for such exemplary conduct is ridiculous! I submit that the only reason for Dr. Blair being brought to trial at all is an effort to find a scapegoat for the tragic events of June twenty-fifth last."

A red-faced man in the audience rose, shook his fist. "He can't be let off that easy!" he shouted. "There was two hundred men killed with Custer! My uncle was one of 'em!" There was a chorus of agreement. People rose, called out. A lady clapped loudly, and someone threw a wadded-up piece of newspaper at Sam. Several men shook their fists and cried, "Hang him!"

"Silence!" Judge Cleary pounded the gavel so hard the polished head flew off and spun into the air. Deprived of the instrument, he rose. "Damn it, shut up—all of you—or I'll have the bailiffs put every last one of you in jail for contempt!"

The hubbub quieted. Muttering, the spectators sat down. A bailiff restored the head to the shank and handed the gavel to the judge.

"Mason!" Judge Cleary ordered, pointing. "Take that man with the big mouth over to the jail and keep him there till I can get around to his case!" Face flushed, he sat down. "I remind you—all of you"—he flourished the gavel like a weapon—"I remind you I will clear this courtroom and conduct this case in private if there is another outburst!" He turned to lawyer Emmett. "Have you finished?"

"I have, sir."

"Then, Mr. Waddell, you may cross-examine the witness."

The prosecutor was pleasant; the outbreak in the courtroom had probably worked to his advantage. Slowly he approached Sam, fingers toying with the gold chain across his vest, looking at the floor as if deep in thought.

"You have told us," he said, "the jury, Judge Cleary—all of us— that you attempted escape."

"I did. And it is the truth!"

Waddell looked up, quizzical. "Yet there has been no evidence offered to support that claim!"

"I wrote it all down in my notebook but—"

"The notebook was left behind, as you told us. So there is no way of proving your claim, is there?"

Sam reddened. "Cletus Wiley could have told you it was true!"

"But the evanescent Mr. Wiley is nowhere to be found."

"I don't know where he is," Sam protested. "He's a trapper, damn it! He could be anywhere!"

Judge Cleary shook his head. "No profanity, please, Dr. Blair!"

"I'm sorry, Your Honor, but—"

"A trapper," Waddell broke in, "whom I understand has several Indian wives and children to boot. I'm afraid Mr. Wiley could hardly be considered a reliable witness."

Sam was about to make an angry reply when from the corner of his eye he saw Emmett shake his head. Frustrated, he sank back in the chair.

"In fact," Mr. Waddell continued, "it is my understanding you yourself have an Indian wife!"

Sam didn't know how the prosecutor had found out and perhaps Waddell was only guessing. He could deny the statement, but denial stuck in his throat. Sweet Grass Woman had indeed been his wife. By now she was probably the mother of his child, without benefit of clergy.

"Yes," he admitted.

There was a stir in the room.

"You are, then," Waddell said smoothly, "what they call a squaw man!"

Sam flushed. "I don't know what they call it! This woman was very kind to me."

"But you lived together, as man and wife?"

"We did. But I don't see what—"

Waddell held up a hand. "You have answered my question. Now let us get on to other matters."

There were more questions, most of which managed to put Sam in a questionable light. He looked helplessly at his lawyer. Emmett was writing on a pad of paper.

Waddell came to his last point. The manner was brisk and cheerful and Sam tensed in his chair.

"In conclusion, Mr. Blair, I must raise a matter which seems to me decisive. The witness Luther Speck testified you snatched a saber away from one of the soldiers—a trooper whom Speck identified as Harmon, Private Billy Harmon."

"I didn't know his name," Sam muttered.

"In any case, Private Harmon, deprived of his weapon, was run through by a Sioux lance and killed. Do you remember Speck's testimony to that effect?"

Sam nodded, throat tight.

"Then it follows, does it not, that you are at the least, the *very* least, an accessory to murder? After all, if Harmon had retained his saber, he probably could have defended himself against the Sioux lance! He could have—"

Sam stood up, pounding fists on the railing surrounding the witness box. "He had just *killed* a man—a boy, really, with that saber! He ran him through and through, and the saber was dripping blood! I'd seen enough blood and killing, and I grabbed it away to stop him!"

Judge Cleary's voice was patient. "Sit down, Dr. Blair. Try to restrain yourself!"

Sam sank into the chair, tears of frustration stinging his eyes.

"Are you all right?" the judge asked. "Are you able to go on?"

Sam took a deep breath, blinked. "Yes, sir." But prosecutor Waddell waved a casual hand, turned away. "I have finished, Your Honor," he announced. "My case has been well established. At any rate, I have no more questions for the defendant."

Judge Cleary had been making notes. For a long time he examined them. From time to time he adjusted the spectacles, thatch of white hair bowed. Spectators shifted in seats, muttered. The courtroom was cold and bleak, and a bailiff put a chunk of wood into the big cast-iron stove. In the witness chair Sam waited, one hand clamped in the other to still the trembling.

The judge raised a shaggy head. "Dr. Blair, I find this a very unusual case—one of great difficulty for all concerned. Much depends on your own attitude, sir—what happened to you, and how you in turn reacted to those influences." He picked up a pencil, rolled it between gnarled fingers. "Now that the prosecutor and defense counsel have summed up, I find myself obliged to depart from precedent and question you myself."

Sam glanced at Emmett, caught a quick flash of warning. *Be careful what you say!*

"As you know," Judge Cleary continued, "the nation has been shocked and saddened by the disaster at the Little Big Horn. How, sir, do you feel about that event?"

Sam bowed his head and spoke in a low voice. "I don't like to see anyone killed, red or white. I'm a—I'm a doctor, Your Honor. My job is to save lives, not destroy them."

"But how do you feel about the Custer incident? What are your personal feelings, Dr. Blair? That is what I am trying to get at."

Sam looked at the judge. "If any human being is killed, I regret it. If two hundred men are killed, my sadness is multiplied by two hundred."

Judge Cleary became impatient. "I am not speaking of a railroad brakeman ground under the cars or of two hundred Chinese drowned in a flood. Those incidents are regrettable; we can all agree on that. But I repeat—what are your *personal* feelings about the Custer massacre?"

Again Sam caught a warning glance from his counsel. Mind in turmoil, he tried to frame a proper response. He saw Clara Wyatt's pale face, eyes dark and circled as she watched. The gaze distracted him. He turned away and saw Jacob Almayer's troubled look. Luther Speck was watching him; John Kelly, Bertha Rambouillet, Major Henry Cushing. But he saw other faces—copper-tinged faces, painted faces, faces hovering over cooking fires, singing faces, faces looking down at nursing babies, watching a wounded white man struggle toward recovery. The wound in his chest still pained him on cold days.

"I don't think it's right to call it a massacre," he murmured.

There was an instant buzz of comment.

"I'm not sure I heard you correctly," Judge Cleary leaned forward, cupping an ear.

"I don't think it's right to call it a massacre, sir. The Indians were camped along the Fat Grass—what white men call the Little Big Horn. All they wanted was to hunt. But they were surprised, and they just defended themselves! They had a lot more men than General Custer did, that's true. But they would have been foolish not to use all they had!"

Judge Cleary pounded his gavel to quiet the clamor.

"All I'm trying to say," Sam blurted, "is that the Sioux weren't looking for trouble! What they wanted to do was hunt, the way they've done every summer for hundreds of years! But they've been pushed back farther and farther. There's no *room* for them to hunt any more! Miners and farmers and the railroads have taken away most of their land, land Government treaties guaranteed them. So what could they do? They're patriots, their own kind of patriots!

They're fighting for their land just like Washington and Jefferson and Franklin did, a hundred years ago!"

He hadn't meant to say so much but it came out in a flood, his voice emotional. There was a look of disaster on lawyer Emmett's face. Mr. Waddell leaned far back in his chair, leg crossed over his knee, with a satisfied look. Judge Cleary sank back, staring at Sam.

"Then, sir, you think Custer and his men got what was coming to them? Is that it?"

"No!" Sam insisted. "That isn't it at all! I'm sad as any American at that awful event!" He groped for words. "What I mean is, the Indians weren't entirely to blame! I mean—"

This time there was no stilling the anger of the spectators. Weary of pounding his gavel, Judge Cleary adjourned court. The bailiffs took Sam back to his cell, quickly, before a crowd could gather in Florence Street. Lawyer Emmett joined him in the jail, upset.

"You're a damned fool!"

Sam took a deep breath. He sat down on the iron cot with its scanty pallet and put his head in hands. "I know!"

"What in hell did you have to blow off like that for?" Emmett paced the narrow confines of the cell. "Here I've worked like a dog to create an acceptable image of you, a picture of a man who just happened to be the victim of an unfortunate situation. Then you utter a few words and blow the whole case to smithereens!" He banged a fist on the table. "Did you see the looks on the faces of the jurors?"

Sam shook his head. "I wasn't looking at them."

"Then you damned well should have been!" Emmett shouted. "We had a chance, a good chance; I could feel it! And you threw it away! Goddamn it, they'll hang you higher 'n Haman!" He kicked at the slop bucket; it spun crazily into a corner. "Waddell was happier than a cat with a platter full of mice!"

"I'm sorry," Sam muttered, "but—"

"Mrs. Wyatt was crying," Emmett growled. "She and her mother both! They knew what it meant!" He sat down on the rickety chair. "Why did you *do* it?"

"I guess I had to be honest."

"Honest?" The lawyer shook his head in disbelief. "At the risk of your neck?"

The turnkey brought a tin plate with fried pork and boiled potatoes, a pot of coffee, some bread. Laying the food on the table, he went out. The lock clicked, a deadly metallic sound.

"At the risk of my neck," Sam said.

"Mind if I pour myself some coffee? My nerves are that jangled!"

"I'm sorry if I caused you trouble," Sam apologized.

"Caused *me* trouble?" Emmett raised bushy eyebrows. Seeing the distraught look on Sam's face, he took a quick sip of coffee. "I'm sorry, too," he muttered. "Here I've been blowing off steam like a rusted-out boiler, and it's not doing anyone any good! I'll have an apoplexy if I don't simmer down!" He took another mouthful of coffee, making a grim face. "Well—" He rose.

"What do we do now?" Sam asked, forlorn.

"Tomorrow old Cleary will charge the jury—you know, go over the details of the case and give them instructions."

"Will I have to be there?"

"No, at this point it's just between the judge and jury. Then the jury will go into session and try to reach a decision. When they've done so, the foreman will notify Judge Cleary. That's when they'll call you back, to hear the verdict."

"How long will it take?" Sam asked.

Emmett shrugged. "Who knows? A day, two days—perhaps only a couple of hours. Depends on what the jurors think of Waddell, you, me." He paused at the cell door. "Sam, I'm sorry I blew up! Didn't mean it. If that's what you had to say, that's what you had to say. You may be a damned fool but you're honest. A lawyer doesn't see too much of that quality nowadays." When the turnkey came, he added, "Is there anything you want or need? Clara—Mrs. Wyatt —gave me extra money just in case. Cigars, a book to read, candles?"

Sam shook his head. "No, thanks, but I appreciate it."

That night he did not sleep. He lay wide-eyed on the cot, staring at the ceiling. Uneaten, the food remained on the tin plate. Cockroaches soon discovered it. From time to time the turnkey looked in, lamp casting shadows on the walls.

"You all right?"

"Yes, thanks."

"Ain't et none of your supper, I see."

"I wasn't hungry."

The turnkey was a kindly man. "It's cold now," he said, "but I could have a man go out and bring you a bowl of soup. You ought to eat, y'know—keep up your strength."

For what? Sam wondered dully. "No," he answered. "I'm all right. Thanks, anyway."

The jury did not take long to reach their verdict. Next morning the guards took Sam back to the courtroom. Feet wet from walking through the snow, he shivered as he sat at the table with lawyer Emmett. "Here," Emmett said. Taking his well-cut woolen coat from the back of a chair, he threw it about Sam's shoulders.

Judge Cleary tapped the gavel.

"Gentlemen, have you reached a verdict?"

The foreman, a tall sallow man with a few strands of hair plastered across a bald skull, cleared his throat. "We have, Your Honor."

"What is your verdict?"

The foreman consulted a crumpled paper.

"We find the defendant guilty as charged."

In the back of the courtroom someone cried out. Heads turned, eyes stared. Clara Wyatt muffled her face in a handkerchief. Assisted by her mother, she quickly left the room.

For a moment the sound of her grief had balked the emotions of the spectators. Now they cheered, applauded, babbled to each other. Judge Cleary watched with weary eyes, saying nothing; he toyed with the gavel but did not use it. Finally he adjourned court. Prosecutor Waddell accepted handshakes, congratulations, predictions of imminent political success. Later, he came over to defense counsel's table and spoke to Sam's disconsolate lawyer.

"Good try, Emmett! For a while you had me worried, though!" He looked at Sam, but did not seem to see him. "I'm sorry, Mr. Blair, but justice was done—I'm sure of that."

Protected by extra guards, Sam was almost dragged through the milling crowds in Florence Street, locked in his cell again. His time, he knew, was running out.

CHAPTER 13

On a chill February morning Judge Cleary asked Sam Blair to rise.

"Dr. Blair," he said, "I want to know if you have anything to say before I pass sentence."

The courtroom was crowded with spectators anxious to hear the penalty for Sam Blair's treasonable conduct. There was, Mr. Emmett had told Sam, a possibility of a long prison sentence, perhaps at hard labor. There was also the death sentence to be kept in mind; Sam should prepare himself. As he rose Emmett muttered something but Sam didn't hear it. Pale from long confinement in the Florence Street jail, he swayed a little, bracing himself with fingers spread on the table.

"Sir?" he asked.

Judge Cleary appeared haggard. The white hair was unkempt. There were dark circles under his eyes.

"Is there anything you would like to say, Dr. Blair?"

Sam stared at a butterfly-shaped ink stain on the rough wood of the table. "I—I—yes, sir, I would like to say a few words."

Judge Cleary leaned back in his chair. "You may proceed."

"Your Honor—" Sam's voice failed. He cleared his throat, started again. "Your Honor, I have got to say I am not guilty of anything, let alone treason. I was always a good citizen, never broke any law I know of. So all I can say is—if I found myself in the same situation again I'd probably do exactly what I did before, and think no less of myself for it. But that's over and done with. The jury found me guilty."

He was not an articulate man, and certainly not religious. But a thought came to him. Perhaps it was unwise to voice it, but he felt impelled.

"General Custer and a lot of good men died a horrible death on the Little Big Horn. I am sorry for them. But white men have tricked and cheated the Indians for a long time. To speak in religious terms, white men have sinned. You all—" For the first time he raised his head. "You've all sinned against other human beings—people who are black or red or any color different from your own, but who still are human beings, creatures of the same God you sing hymns to on Sunday. And so—I've got to say it—like the man called Jesus, I'm crucified for your sins!"

Pandemonium broke out in the courtroom. There were cries of "Blasphemer!" Spectators shook fists at Sam Blair, shouted imprecations, clamored for an immediate noose. To no avail Judge Cleary pounded his gavel. Finally he signaled the bailiffs to clear the courtroom. Protesting, the crowd was herded out.

"Sacrilege, that's what it is!" a stout matron screamed, struggling with a bailiff. "How can the judge let him say such things?" A fat man being shoved through a doorway turned and snarled. "I don't want to stay in this courtroom anyway! Pretty quick the good Lord's gonna hurl a lightning bolt down and destroy the whole damned place!"

The only people allowed to remain were newspaper correspondents. Sam saw Mr. Roland busily scribbling. The other reporters—St. Louis *Globe-Democrat*, Denver *Rocky Mountain News*, San Francisco *Chronicle*—were likewise occupied, avid for the sensational story. *He called himself Jesus!* Sam winced.

"Dr. Blair," Judge Cleary said. He leaned on his elbow, pinching the bridge of his nose between his fingers, eyes closed.

"Yes, sir."

"I have thought for a long time about this case—whether the jury's verdict was just, what sentence I should pass. To use another biblical parallel, I had my own Gethsemane. I do not intend that to be sacrilegious any more than I think your reference to the Crucifixion was blasphemous. I was sorely tried, as I think you were, sir."

The courtroom was silent, the only sound the scratching of pens on paper, a muted murmur from the crowds gathered below in Florence Street, the grinding wheels of a dray wagon.

"I know the uses of mercy, Dr. Blair. As a judge, I am often constrained to think on mercy, and a judge is never sure of the justice of his decision. But the law is clear. You committed treason, according to that law, against these United States. So"—Judge Cleary picked up the worn gavel and examined it as if finding reassurance in the polished wood—"I now sentence you to be transported by federal marshals to Fort Pike, in that same Idaho Territory where your treasonable acts were committed. There, on March seventh, in the year of our Lord eighteen hundred and seventy-seven, you will be hanged by the neck until dead."

Sam felt giddy. The room reeled; he was grateful for his counsel's steadying hand.

"It's not over yet!" Emmett whispered hoarsely. "We'll appeal!"

Back in his cell, Sam shook his head in disbelief. "I don't understand it. Somehow I've been caught up in a thing that's bigger than I am! I'm a national figure! Yet all I ever wanted was to be a good doctor, treating people, comforting the sick and dying, relieving pain." Helplessly he gestured. "Mr. Emmett, I'm not *right* for this! Doesn't it seem to you it takes a great character, King Lear or Hamlet, to stand on a national stage like this, spouting speeches, saying things that will go down in history? But I'm not that kind of a person! So what in hell am I doing here in jail, with the newspapers full of headlines about me?"

Emmett shrugged. "Something touched you, Sam—I don't know what! But we all have to be ready to play whatever role the Good Lord asks us to play."

The days passed, long, long days, while the appeals went up the ladder of courts. Emmett brought Sam reading matter; *Harper's Weekly*, the *National Police Gazette*, Frank Leslie's *Illustrated Weekly Newspaper*. Some sections were missing, items scissored out. From kindness Emmett had probably deleted those portions he judged might prove distressing. But Sam learned that General Miles, his soldiers clad in warm buffalo coats, was slashing across the one-time Sioux lands in pursuit of Sitting Bull and his miscreants. Sioux ammunition, it was reported, was exhausted. Miles was burning villages, destroying stocks of food, killing great numbers of Sioux warriors, herding women and children onto the reservations. *Where is she?* Sam wondered—Sweet Grass Woman and the child, his child?

In March, Emmett came to his cell. His face was somber.

"Last appeal denied. The Supreme Court decided the trial was proper, the decision fair." Angry, he crushed his hat and flung it at the wall. "Damn it, they rushed those appeals through like they were going to a fire! The whole thing was undignified, even lewd—not worthy of the law I served all these years!"

Sam felt a great weight pressing down on him. "I'm sure you did all you could, Mr. Emmett," he said. "It was just—just the times, I guess."

"The times!" Lawyer Emmett recovered his hat, straightened the brim. "The times!" he repeated bitterly. "The law is supposed to be *above* the times!"

Samuel Penrose Blair was hanged at Fort Pike, Idaho Territory, on April 26, 1877. Major Henry Cushing, his face somber, carried out the mandate of the courts. A 7th Cavalry chaplain, a Roman Catholic priest, talked to Mr. Oscar Roland of the Chicago *Daily News* after the execution, from which reporters had been barred.

"He seemed very calm. I prayed with him for a long time in his cell. Somehow, he did not seem to be paying much attention to me. He talked in a strange language."

"Sioux, probably," Roland said. He blew his nose. "Blair lived with them for a long time. Had an Indian wife; it came out at the trial."

"Only at the last," Father Bryan told him, "did he speak in English. As they were putting the hood over his head, he said 'I have a son.' 'A son?' I asked. I didn't know he had a son. I thought he was unmarried. 'Yes,' Dr. Blair said. 'I have a son. Maybe someday he can do what I tried to do. God have mercy on us, red and white alike.' Then he just stood there, patient and dignified, till the trap was sprung."

Major Cushing intended to bury the body in an unmarked grave at the outskirts of Fort Pike to avoid contamination of the brave military dead who lay in the post cemetery. But at the last moment an old man in buckskins appeared and claimed the remains. No one remembered his name. Henry Cushing, years later, recalled the picture of the grizzled old man leading his pony westward into a spring sky, the body limp across the high-backed Sioux saddle.

BIBLIOGRAPHY

1. Bourke, John G. *On the Border with Crook*. New York: Charles Scribner's Sons, 1891
2. Brown, Dee. *Bury My Heart at Wounded Knee*. New York: Holt, Rinehart and Winston, 1970
3. Clark, W. P. *Indian Sign Language*. Philadelphia: Hamersly & Co., 1885
4. DeBarthe, Joe. *Life and Adventures of Frank Gruard*. Norman, Oklahoma: University of Oklahoma Press, 1958
5. Grinnell, George Bird. *The Cheyenne Indians; Their History and Way of Life*. New York: Cooper Square Publishers Inc., 1962
6. *The Indians* (*The Old West*). New York: Time-Life Books, 1973
7. Marquis, Thomas B. *Keep the Last Bullet for Yourself*. New York: Two Continents Publishing Group Inc., 1976
8. *Pioneer Atlas of the American West*. San Francisco: Rand McNally and Co., 1956